I0547907

The Bohemian Guide to Monogamy

Andrew Armacost

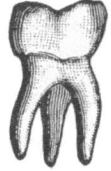

Bizarro Pulp Press
an imprint of JournalStone Publishing

Bizarro Pulp Press books may be ordered through booksellers or by contacting:

Bizarro Pulp Press, a JournalStone imprint
   www.BizarroPulpPress.com

The views expressed in this work are solely those of the authors and do not necessarily reflect the views of the publisher, and the publisher hereby disclaims any responsibility for them.

   ISBN: 978-1-942712-62-6

Printed in the United States of America
JournalStone rev. date: October 24, 2015

   Cover Art: Matthew Revert
      www.matthewrevert.com
   Interior Formatting: Lori Michelle
      www.theauthorsalley.com

To Pederson

"Promiscuity is like never reading past the first page. Monogamy is like reading the same book over and over."
—Mason Cooley

Warming Up

(Part 1)

Before the weirdness starts and the madness hijacks my story, before the words congeal into a pimp-slap to the psyche, let me start, dear inquisitive reader, by first setting the scene . . .

The colonnaded mansion across the street is drenched in Georgia sunshine. And all along the sidewalk everyone seems to be squinting or else wearing sunglasses.

It's really warming up.

Here at The Oglethorpe Café, your beleaguered narrator sits at a small cedar table that wobbled until I jammed a few napkins under its one malingering leg.

Savannah, well, it's such an enchanting little city. And I can see it all from here: dogs being walked through the square, a statue of some stoical confederate general on a horse, wrought iron fences, tenements with shops below and balconies above. All this, and the sky seems almost surreal, otherworldly. I mean, it's the kind of clear blue sky that Hollywood would manufacture for a big-budget musical. Ah yes, it's a bliss-filled slice of utopian Americana, right here before my squinting eyes. But it's not blue skies or the goddamned golden sunshine that's on my mind this afternoon . . .

First of all, every time I sit down to write something lately I get— I don't know, I guess I've been feeling a bit frustrated . . . vitiated, depressed . . . insipid, obfuscated . . . bamboozled, run-amok . . . grouchy, shitty, pissy . . . conflicted and almost totally suffocated.

It fucks you up, a family does . . . it does not mean to but it does . . .
Drains the juice.

9

Desiccates one's mojo.

A family giveth, and taketh.

(And taketh.)

My wife, Fumiko, seated here to my right (almost on top of me), is reading about—well, I have no idea what she's reading—something in Japanese. But let me guess . . . it's about Romantic love with a great big R? Yes, of course. Or one of its conduits. She only reads serious works at night. Her daytime reading is pure provender. Either I've been misled for many years, or this moment is about as close as it gets to her version of a real-life Paradiso:

* Romance novel.
* Adoring husband.
* Anniversary weekend.
* Cloudless sky.
* The first café we stopped in during our honeymoon, replete with a walk down Memory Lane.

Yep, pretty close to Shangri-La, right baby?

This morning, Fumiko braided her long onyx hair into pigtails to go with her short plaid skirt. She's looking a bit naughty for me today, a bit schoolgirl. And obviously pregnant. "One and one on the way," as they say. Except in this case they'd be wrong. We have two on the way, identical twin boys. And our little girl Eva in the stroller here, she's mercifully sawing logs.

How, I still wonder, did I ever become that guy? That guy with the minivan at the end of the cul-de-sac. Home insurance. Life insurance. Health insurance. Additional insurance in case the primary insurance doesn't cut it. An extremely boring wardrobe. Boring friends. Boring job. Boring conversations. Asleep by nine-thirty on a Friday. How'd it happen?

Well, when I finally finished my contract with the navy, I taught English in Kyoto for a year, by which I mean I dropped out of life for a while and didn't do much. Fumiko had been one of my many lackluster students. Until she got pregnant. Now I sell copy machines in Indianapolis. I sell a lot of them and so we do okay. We get by.

Of course, I look at her sometimes and I'm suddenly overwhelmed with love and appreciation and, okay, occasionally some awe. I do lots of "little things" for which the American Disciples of Oprah would surely applaud me. Flowers, feet rubs . . . I'm full service. Oh, I'm a diaper changing daddy, and I drink only in moderation, only on the weekends. I scrub toilets. Since our marriage, I've discovered the Roth, the 401K, and the 529 for college.

Now wash all that down with a mortgage and a dog that still shits right in the middle of the living room floor and we see how natural it is for the formula of life to supplant one's will to create. The whole thing just sneaks up on you and pretty soon your life isn't yours. It's all been hijacked.

OKAY, here's a new but soon to be related subject . . .

It's deplorable when a novelist tries to actively seduce Hollywood rather than just sort of, I don't know, letting it happen. The instant you crack open this sort of book, this garbage, you get a good strong whiff of it. And you know. This thing is a screenplay masquerading as a novel. It's like that first bite of a Big Mac, when you realize Hey, wait a second . . . this ain't f o o d.

Still . . . I covet filmmakers because they're able to instantly and quite literally flesh out their characters with real honest-tuh-goodness Homo sapiens. Most novelists sacrifice soooooo many pages in an often futile attempt to bring Homo make-believus to life in the minds of the reader. Yes, we endow these made-up people with hair, eyes, teeth, lips, shoes, good habits, bad habits, ways of walking, talking, knocking on a door, et cetera, and so on . . .

Naturally, the reader can easily get bogged down in all this detail and still not have a decent idea of what a character would look like if he or she were to walk through that door right now.

Maybe it's time to stand this dilemma on its head. After all, the saprophytic film industry has been pilfering Literature for decades now; it's about time for writers to get something back, you know, about time for us to be on top for once.

So from now on, I'm casting BIG name stars into my pages. It'll save me headaches and keep the reader moving forward with very little effort.

Jesus. It's really warming up, and my fricken food is still AWOL. Consequently, I'm a bit lightheaded.

Anyway, it's past eleven now. Time to start the auditions . . .

TAKE ONE

Garcon, I say to a tall pimply creature sporting a ludicrous under-bite; a physics/accounting double major currently struggling through the second year of his undergraduate studies, I'm guessing. Numbnuts, as we shall call him, sprints to our table with an almost heel-clacking servility and bleats,

—Sir?

—Yeah, when the soup's ready, could you serve that up with a portion of Pamela Anderson?

—Of course sir, he says with a droopy grin—Something from the Silicone Valley epoch?

—Yeah, uhhh . . . nineteen-ninety-six should work, I guess.

—Excellent choice sir. Very good year, he says, bowing at the waist. He asks if there's anything else he can do for us. When I tell him there's nothing I can think of, the flatfooted yutz kahclumps his way to the kitchen.

Meanwhile, the overlapping conversations on the patio conflate into one garbled voice that is itself a form of silence. Like the first moments of arousal when the blood starts to flow into the right places, ideas begin to swirl around me and I can feel myself headed toward a writer's state of mind, a space where stuff disconnects, flows freely, then reconnects in unexpected ways. For some reason, the Superman archetype keeps popping into my dome. Images from my youth. Comic strips. Cartoons. Dolls for boys, like G.I. Joe. Using a red bath towel as a cape, chasing my babysitter over the furniture.

Thoughts and feelings, memories and words; they rain down on me like sharpened metal from an Apache-filled sky as my pen pirouettes across the page. This sublime alienation amid society is suddenly shorn as Numbnuts returns and, in so doing, nearly dumps a cup of coffee on my wife's lap. Naturally, I start berating our well-intentioned dolt. But then he swiftly finds forgiveness, friends, because the soup might be cold but Pammy is hot. H-O-T-T hot-hot. She's wearing that bright red one-piece number that so deftly brought her fame, well before the hepatitis and that sorry-ass Tommy Lee video of Internet infamy.

I order our freshly baked automaton to remove her bathing suit, which she does . . . and with a broad, provocative smile no less. I indicate that it might be best if she sat to my left (Fumiko being to my right).

Granted, this isn't the real Pamela Anderson. Had the real Pamela Anderson been cast into my pages against her will, goodness, I might get sued for defamation of character, or slander, perhaps . . . or really, just about anything (this being America). No, the character before you has been inspired by the visage of a familiar Hollywood star. That's all. Nothing less. But certainly nothing more. This Pamela looks almost precisely—but not quite exactly—just like the Pamela we know from TV (and yes, the Internet).

Bizarro Pam, we may call her. She has a life of her own now.

Like a hungry kitten to a warm saucer of milk, Pam scoot-scoot-scoots her metal chair closer to mine and says—OmyGawd OmyGawd, I totally can't believe it's you, Scotty. I must be dreaming, right? Somebody pinch me!

—Pam, look, if I wanted something other than ocular junk food, I mean, if the female lead was supposed to speak very much, do you honestly think you'd be in the running? I probably would've gone with Isabelle Huppert at her peak, or maybe Naomi Watts— anyway, you get the point. What I have in mind for you is not exactly a speaking role. Ah, but Beauty is its own passport, and you're proving that right now by your simple presence, your mystifying fame. Oh, Pammy. Come now. Tuck that lower lip back in. I'm just giving you a hard time. A little grief. Now here's what I have so far; you mind reading this out loud for us?

Then I hand her the pad of paper I've been doodling on and she just sort of, I don't know, goes blank behind those deep blue contact lenses as she battles with her first line—Hi, my name's Bizarro Pam. I'm frozen in time. I never grow old. I'm twenty-seven forever and my hobbies include m-mal . . . mala . . . malap . . .

Andrew Armacost

—Malapropisms and Sapphic scatology, I say, but I'm too impatient to deal with this, so I inveigle our bleach blond automaton to slide under the table, where she's apt to be much more suitably employed. While Pam gets comfortable under there, I pop another piece of nicotine gum. I told the wife I'd quit smoking if she ever got pregnant again. She did. So I'm trying.

Well the gum just ain't cuttin' it, I must confess. It's . . . it's double-condom sex, freshwater scuba, John Lennon orchestrated for an elevator, imitation leather, sushi at a mall, jail-time sans la reach-around, music without vicissitudes, life without the high notes. This fucking sucks.

Whilst I fondle Pam's twenty-seven-year-old marmoreal breasts beneath the table, Fumiko uses a long red fingernail to reserve her spot on the page and looks at me with one of those spousal smiles that mean a million things at once: thank you again for the ring, I love it . . . do you think I should cut my hair? . . . thanks for always taking out the trash, I do notice these things my sweet sweet honey . . . I won't interrupt you while you're writing but when you find a convenient stopping point I'd like to touch base on something . . . probably something I've already told you at least once but would like to reiterate because I'm so fond of reiteration and because you have such a poor employment record as a listener but I love you anyway.

Well, when I'm writing dirt—that is, when one wishes to coalesce the strident vapors of the mind's darker shadow self—the last thing I need is a moist pair of Bambi eyes pressed against my conscience. It's like playing chess on magic mushrooms, or trying to masturbate with an overzealous mime in the room. Just doesn't work.

I acquiesce to her kryptonite gaze and land a loud peck on Fumiko's scantily perfumed neck, just below the earlobe. We nuzzle. We separate.

Meanwhile, Pam's off to the races. A real thoroughbred, this one. I glance at Fumiko to see if she's privy to my fantasy life. Nope. Quietly reading. Oblivious to the inside of my skull.

Good.

The juices are starting to flow, you know, things are really warming up as I feed the maggots in my head. Munch, munch, munch.

Now I'm o-O-O-o!!! . . . gripping the

14

edge of the table with both hands. White knuckles. Tightly flexed ass muscles. And a face, ah-h-h, like you just bit a lemon. Finally there's this, I don't know, fainting sensation as I pump out all that anxiety, frustration, and writer's block. Out comes the first story:

Superman Searches
for His Smile

About a year ago, things started going south between Lois and me.

Lois, well, she's always been competitive, driven, even difficult at times, but until recently, her tenacity was tempered by a fundamental goodness, a sublimated softness that, to me, made Lois *Lois*.

I don't know where we jumped the tracks, exactly. I just know that somewhere something changed, something broke. She grew impatient with me. Far less understanding. Less forgiving. Even spiteful. Now she brazenly picks at my insecurities, furtively drawing attention to my adoptive roots, my early beginnings as an orphan, dredging up all my suppressed fears of abandonment, intimacy, and emotional inadequacy, even using this collective fear to hurt me intentionally. In a word, she's become inexplicably *cruel*.

Still, I could never leave Lois. I love her as nothing else. At this point, I find it difficult to imagine a life without Lois, which seems tantamount to a life without life, more or less.

Well it all began soon after my proposal. We'd been engaged less than a week when I noticed the change, when she soured toward me, when her face took on a permanent scowl. Naturally I told myself that Lois was merely experiencing pre-marital anxiety. She had the jitters, I decided. That's all. Cold feet.

Time passed but nothing improved. We've been engaged six months and yet nothing's gotten better. I've done all I can to keep us together, biting my lip, enduring her tirades, her lectures, her snide remarks, her insults and her unexplainable hatefulness. I'm exhausted and she refuses to get some counseling with me. She seems committed to *not* trying. How long, I wonder, will this go on?

With the holidays fast approaching, Lois finally dumped me, made a nice clean break (clean from her perspective); she threw all my stuff out on the curb, including my cape, which I just had dry-cleaned. Then she un-friended me on Facebook after giving poor Krypto to the pound and calling me a "single-minded workaholic."

"You're right," I conceded, trying to fish out my iPhone from the bottom of the toilet, "I need a better work/life balance. Let's go someplace this weekend so we can talk. Just you and me, what do you say?"

"I say the only thing super about you is your ego!"

"Lois, *baby* . . ."

"Don't 'Lois, baby' me. I'll be back in a week. Have the rest of your super-shit outta here by Monday."

"Where are you going?"

She gave me a sarcastic laugh, throwing the door open with an almost sadistic brio. I began to beg but she was already halfway to the elevator, hauling a suitcase behind her.

I knew she was serious this time, that some straw—forgetting her birthday?—had apparently broken the beleaguered camel's back. She even blocked my number, plus every email address I'd ever used.

So. It was over. I couldn't believe it . . . but then, I did believe it.

By December I was really blue. Depressed is the word, I guess. So depressed, incidentally, that I hadn't stopped a single crime in over a week. I watched a shoplifter pocket some malt liquor at the 7/11 and didn't say a word. I quit going to the gym, quit showing up at the Friday pep rallies over at the Justice League Fraternal Lodge.

Lois, I soon found out, had left her desk at the paper to take a job as an anchorwoman for Fox News. I spent whole evenings staring at the tube, hoping to catch one glimpse of her face, which, these days, was plastered over with a thick mask of makeup.

Aquaman was growing concerned, apparently. The morning

after Christmas, he stopped over and found me sleeping in my wrinkled costume, passed out in front of a CSI rerun, disheveled and unshaven.

There was a pungent smell—twelve-year scotch, mixed with aging salmon—a smell so strong that it woke me up. I knew it was him.

"What do you want?" I said, rolling over on my side, crushing the remote control with my ribs.

"Dude, what happened to your nose?"

"Don't fly drunk. That's all I can say."

"You look like shit warmed over."

"Thanks."

"You know what you need?"

"Yeah," I said. "Lois. But it's too late now, so please just scram. And shut the door on the way out this time."

"Oh forget Lois," he said, as if her very name was absurd. "Man, what you need is Pattaya Beach."

"What kind of a beach?"

"It's in Thailand."

"Oh. Why Thailand?"

"Don't ask. Just go. It's the answer to your un-prayed prayers."

Aquaman helped himself to whatever was left in my refrigerator and then sat down beside me, eating cold vegan pizza in my ear. He kept going on and on—Thailand this and Thailand that—until I found myself thinking . . . Well, what the hell, it's worth a shot.

Along the way, I saved a crew of stranded sailors and still made it to Pattaya Beach in less than five hours. Thailand. The Land of Smiles. So this was it.

My face was wind-burnt. Over the North Pole, I had somehow lost a new red leather boot, an expensive one. And my debit card had fallen out of my belt somewhere over Shanghai. But otherwise I was feeling okay . . . maybe a little jet-lagged, or cape-lagged, or whatever.

For two weeks I sat by the pool all alone, getting blitzed on beer and beach drinks. I read a little, here and there, and devoted most evenings to feeling sorry for myself.

I thought constantly of Lois. What was she doing? Where was she sleeping? Given her bottomless reservoir of talent, why was she working for Fox News? What was she wearing, eating, thinking? Did she think about me? It was driving me nuts.

At night, I did some Thai boxing to earn a little pocket money until my new debit card showed up in the mail. Besides, it helped me blow off steam. Beer and boxing. That was pretty much it for two weeks straight. Then I wandered into the business lounge, discovering that some knucklehead had left his email open, and it got me thinking . . .

###

Date: Thu, 11 Mar 2015 20:34:18 +0000 (GMT)
From: Biancaarst@dlhl.com.au
Subject: Fwd: FW: Fwd: FW: RE: **Translated from Thai**
To: jkuisel_babyspice@yahoo.com,   okoh80@yahoo.co.uk, barbacoa@hotmail.co.uk, jjmiller@dlhl.co.uk
SEEN THIS ONE?
MORE WEDDING PICS ON THE WAY.
MISSSSSSSSSSSSS YOUUUUUUUUUUUUUUU GIRLSSSS LOOOOOOOOOADS!!!!!!!

BIANCS

David Arst <davarst@patrickdef.com.au> wrote:
From: Davarst@patrickdef.com.au
To: "Bianca Baby"
Subject: FW: Fwd: FW: RE: Translated from Thai
Date: Wed, 11 Mar 2014 20:32:24 +0000
Biancs,
Q: Guess what?
A: Chicken-butt!
How ya going sweetness? Hope your day's less hectic than mine!
I just got this email from a mate of mine in Thailand. It's been making me think about you *all day*: not that I don't think about you all day *every* day.
See you at home. Love you!

Love,
David
PS. More.

>From: Andrew Salisbury
>To: Davarst@patrickdef.com.au
>Subject: Fwd: FW: RE: Translated from Thai
>Date: Wed, 10 Mar 2014 20:20:45 +0000 (GMT)
>
>Arst,
>
>Greetings from the land-of-smiles my brother. Check out this note from a buddy of mine I used to work with. Good guy. Totally hit me in the gut. How's Oz? How's the new crib?

>NBL,
>Sals
>Simon Tonini wrote:
>From: Simon Tonini
>To: Ansalisbury@slovo.co.th
>Subject: FW: RE: Translated from Thai
>Date: Wed, 10 Mar 2015 08:16:04 +0000
>
>
>
>Andrew,
>
>I received a note from Jim that I believe was intended for you as well. Please see me when you return from lunch. Thank you.
>
>R,
>
>Simon
    >
    >
    >
    > From: James Ratcliff
    > To: Stonini@slovo.co.th

> Subject: RE: Translated from Thai
> Date: Tue, 09 Mar 2015 18:55:52 -0800 (PST)
>
> >Sorry. Can't seem to get it to attach properly. A copy of her letter is pasted below:
>_____
>

> >James,
>
> >
>
> >I am writing this in my language now, with the intention of having it translated as soon as possible. I am not hiding behind a letter, I plan to read this to your face.
> >
>
> >I CAN read English.
>
> >I am writing this in my language first, so for once you'll understand me.
>
> >I left my friends and family. I left my home and everything I knew so I could be with you. I want to say you owe me nothing but that is just not true.
>
> >A chance. It's what I took on you, I need the same. I deserve the same.I said it. Deserve. You owe me this.
> >
>
> > You get frustrated when I can't remember Newton's Second Law or Adam Smith's "Invisible Hand" or the hidden meaning inside some dusty novel. If you wanted an encyclopedia instead of honestly and devotion . . . if you wanted a woman that could blab on and on in English and knock your friends over with her brain, then why did you marry me?
>
> >No one MADE you propose and no one made you make

promises. Maybe you just wanted a piece of Asia to take back with you, something that could almost fit in your carry-on luggage to remind you of where and what you had been. But I am not some wooden doll from a curio shop and never will be. I am a human being. A man that confuses things with people is a bad man. He is not a man.

>

>

> >But you are not a bad man Jim, or at least you do not want to be or mean to be. Or at least I do not think so, or else I would not waste the ink and anguish.

>

>

> >You encourage me to talk more at dinners and parties, and when I do you look embarrassed and make excuses for me when I go to the bathroom (and cry—did you know that?).

> >

>

> > You rub my face in books like a master would rub his dog's nose in a mess and now I hate the way they smell.

>

>

> > When we met, you were one of the good westerners. Not loud or rude or disrespectful. Never arrogant. Good-hearted, and you at least TRIED to learn Thai. I am not the one who changed

>

>

> > America has not been what you promised. You never told me I would need pepper-spray on my keychain. You never told me I would touch so many lifeproof plastic things. It has not been paradise Honey but see, I never thought it would be. I knew the stains of dreams would wash away and leave a new reality . . . a reality I THOUGHT we would be facing together. But you are not facing it, you are turning away. You still expect the dream, don't you? You want what I WAS and what I AM BECOMING and what I WILL BE and you want them all now, all at the same time.

>

>

> > You get frustrated when I do not understand or do not like the poetry you read to me. All that blah blah blah dah dah dah about love and sacrifice and eternal devotion . . . poems written about passing seasons that were never meant to last, written by dead failed lovers who only succeeded in creating false expectations for the rest of us.

>

> > Then last night it occurred to me . . . you are not worth tears if you are so blind as to miss the poem in front of you. She lives with you, feels for you, cooks for you, rubs your temples, warms your bed, always supports you and always listens. Your poem is trying to understand you and needs YOU to TRY to understand.

>

>

> > You are older than me. I am healthier than you. Always, we have known this. But no matter what happens, as long as you really love me, I would never leave you. I would always stand by you, just like we promised in your big marble church.

> > .

>

>

> > When I started this letter, I was not certain what I needed to say. Now I am.

>

>

> > I will never abandon you Jim, on one condition. You must love me on love's terms and not on your own. You must love me and I must know it. Remain patient and kind and try to understand. I will always do my best but you must stop looking down on me. I love you and most likely, I always will.

>

>

> > BUT

>

>
> > You must learn to look me in the eye, not down at me. Otherwise, I am leaving forever.
>
>
> >With Love and Dignity,
>
> >
>
> > Mookda
>

> From: Simon Tonini
>
> >To: jamratclif@slovo.com
>
> >Subject: RE: Translated from Thai
>
> >Date: Mon, 08 Mar 2004 14:07:52 -0800 (PST)
> >
> >
>
> >Jim,
>
> >
>
> > I'm terribly sorry, was there supposed to an attachment to this email?
>

> > James Ratcliff wrote:
>
> >
>
> > >From: James Ratcliff
>
> > >To: Stonini@slovo.co.th
>
> > >Subject: Translated from Thai
>

> > >Date: Mon, 08 Mar 2015 11:58:35 -0800 (PST)
>
> > >
>
> > >Simon,
>
> > > I wanted to call and thank again for making it here but somehow I forgot to pay the phone bill and I seem to have misplaced my cell. Been a bit distracted, as you may imagine but wanted you to know how very much I apprecaite your support.
>
> > > Anyway, look, this is a bit difficult but I feel there's soemthing I need to share with you. Not sure where to begin. I know that you and Nong are thinking about moving home next year and I just wanted to share something with you before you attempt the transition.
>
> > > When i found Mookda, next to her body there was a note written in Thai. Apparently, she'd written it after our last tiff, with the intention of having it translated. I dont know and I guess I will never know what finally pushed her over the edge. It wasn't infidelity, i can assure you, or any one event I don't think.
>
> > >Of coursel had the letter translated and have since read it many many times, as you may imagine. Most the advice offered to me is useless to me now, which makes me sad some days and angry others, for having not been given the chance to try. But I thought you might benefit from it. You and Nong. If you think any of the other guys would benefit from it, feel free to pass it along—I dont think my circumstances are much of a mystery.
>
> > > Not sure how to close this one Simon. Pls tell Nong I said hello. Let's look for something other than a funeral to bring us together again soon.
>

> > > Thank you again for everything.
>
> > >
>
> > > Deepest regards,
>
> > > Jim
>
>
> > >————————————————————

Week 3 at the pool.

I was getting pretty burnt and my ass was hurting from the plastic poolside furniture. I couldn't take it anymore, the whole act of wallowing in my own pity. At some point, the very feat of feeling sorry for myself actually took more energy than all other options. I had OP'd, I had over-pitied.

So one day I finally got up, went to the room, did five thousand pushups in less than a minute, took a quick shower, and then headed out toward Walking Street after shot-gunning a beer from the mini-fridge.

Next, it was into a "baht-bus" with the rest of the Pattaya Beach sleaze; what a collection of perverts, perhaps the single largest congregation of deformed personalities on Earth. And that's saying a lot. Ah yes, the Gary Glitters of the world, all gathered together. Those shit-birds, they were lucky I was off-duty.

Walking Street is an X-rated version of Bizarro World.

Beer bar to beer bar, my buzz gained momentum. Stepping out of some tin-roofed hovel, I noticed that the sun was setting, giving the sky a nice, soothing, beer-like quality. Up above, I noticed a half-naked white lady dancing in this gigantic fishbowl of a window. White chicks? In Pattaya? I had to check this out.

No cover at the door. Red fabric on the walls . . . cheap but ornate furniture . . . silky lampshades. And women, young ones. Of legal age, I think, but still pretty creepy for my taste. Ukrainians and Russians, mostly, with a couple of Africans thrown in.

I was offered a seat on a smallish couch toward the back, next to a young thin blond woman wearing a crushed red velvet dress. I bought her a twenty dollar drink. She put her arm around my neck. Her flesh was icy.

"Vere you come from?" She said, half-yawning as her moon-colored eyes grew moist with boredom.

"Ohio," I lied, thereby dodging the whole planet-far-away discussion.

"Amereeka?"

"Canada," I lied again, hoping to avoid yet another half-educated anti-American rant.

"Canada is cold, yes? Like my motherland."

We talked for a while but I just wasn't into it. The whole thing felt too, I don't know, transactional. After years of brainwashing myself into always doing the right thing, I needed to be lied to, gently eased into the act of self-deception, after which, I figured, everything else should play out logically and I could finally alleviate a certain mind-altering case of blue balls. Still, I wasn't ready for something as cold-blooded as a pump-and-dump with this ice-cold Ukrainian whore, so I got up and left her there mid-sentence.

Some goon at the door stopped me and I thought there was a problem, I thought I was in trouble. I wasn't. All he wanted was an autograph for his kid.

"I'm not him."

"You *are* him. I know you are *him*."

"Fine," I said, then I signed a glossy photo of me lifting up a Toyota SUV in Brooklyn in the hopes of saving a mother and daughter (the mother made it . . . the daughter, well, it still rips me up).

Outside, in the street, I stood there for a while and took it all in . . . whorehouse, go-go bar, boxing ring, tailor shop, young whore, old whore, future whore. The whole scene left me awestruck and vaguely sad. Suddenly Kansas seemed so very far away.

Standing there rudderless like that, I got pulled into a sex show. Not my cup of depravity, as it turns out. So I stepped outside and bought a pack of smokes. I lit one up using my laser vision. Some tourist on a scooter did a double-take, nearly crashing into a telephone pole. It was the first cigarette in my life and it went down perfectly with my growing beer buzz. I should've started years ago.

Around this time, the whole thing sucked me under. Booze? Cigarettes? Bar girls? This was a new low. It made last year's low look like a record-setting high.

I drank as if I had a super-human liver, which of course I do . . . whiskey, beer, more whiskey . . . from one bar to the next, until, half-conscious, half-crazy, I stumbled into a dump where the waitresses wore these sexy nurse uniforms with pink bikini bottoms. The topless girls on stage were young, brown, thin, and beautiful, each with a numbered tag dangling from her panties—meaning, I surmised, you could order them up like cattle.

Okay, look. I was drunk, horny, lonesome, and quickly approaching a nervous breakdown. I deserved a little company. Superman was super-depressed. So I called a girl down from the stage, the one with the big fake tits. I knew they were fake because, using my X-ray vision, I could see those silicone pouches. She said something I could barely hear over the music, over "Cookie," by R. Kelly:

"What your name is?"

"Kevin," I replied, flashing half a smile.

"You strong strong sexy man."

We struggled through this painful, low-English rigmarole. She sat on my lap and spoke to me like Jar Jar Binks.

Since the breakup with Lois, I'd grown sick with physical desire. The time had come, I decided . . . or, more accurately, I simply stopped fighting that caveman impulse.

The waitress came over to take my order. She looked familiar. And so she was. It was Chai-Lai, some girl I rescued about nine months ago, back in Long Beach, where I found her in a shipping container full of human cargo, brought over by a Bulgarian mob boss nicknamed "The Wrench," a half-human monster who ran a ring of underground sweatshops stretching from Orange County all the way up to Bremerton.

I hadn't recognized her in the nurse outfit. Besides which, she'd done something to her hair . . . it was wavy now, and dyed dark black instead of chestnut brown. Or maybe that was its natural color. She was all made up. In her nose she wore a tiny fake diamond. I was hoping she had a navel ring to go with it.

"Superman!" she said with a gasp.

"Pipe down, honey. Just call me Clark, all right?"

"Clark?"

"Yeah," I said, nearly throwing the other girl off my lap as I stood up. "So what the hell are you doing in a place like this?"

"Working. Need money now."

"Yeah, sure, but here?"

"After they arrest me, and send me back from USA . . . what to do?"

"My bad," I said, feeling guilty now. "I never meant to involve those ICE agents. They mean well but . . . "

"You want beer?"

"Sit down," I said, patting the bar stool.

"Must work, Super Clark."

"Please, it's just plain old Clark."

"Clark, I must work for now."

"Okay, well . . . how much is your fee, or whatever? Let's go someplace decent."

She tilted her head to one side, looking all offended. A waitress isn't a hooker. I think that's what she meant to say. But then I found the madam, the boss; I gave her two hundred bucks and we were off.

Down the street a ways, we took an outdoor table at a seaside Mexican joint called Panchito's . . . I poked around at a plate of soggy tacos while Chai-Lai nailed me with a heart-wrenching sob story about her father's cancer, her brother's gambling, and the family's water buffalo, which had just keeled over in the middle of a rice paddy.

"I'm all alone now," she said to me softly, a silent plea welling up in her eyes.

"Ditto," I said. "Lois left me."

"I know," she said. "The Internet told me."

"Jesus. So it's already out there???"

"I don' like see you sad. Make me sad," she said in a quiet voice, embroidered with that sing-song accent. And then she gave me a glance that grew into a gaze.

"It's late," I said, throwing down some cash for the tacos and beer. "I better take off."

We never discussed what was going on between us. But out in the street, when I turned right toward my room at the Marriott, Chai-Lai took my hand and followed after, skipping like a school girl.

In the elevator, we got right to it, started kissing and grabbing and slurping . . . going at it like blue-skinned avatars on the planet of Pandora, hissing and biting. Much like myself, it was out of this world.

The elevator opened. I scurried down the hall, pulling her along. I couldn't get the key to work so I just ripped away the entire knob. Off it went. Put it on my bill.

The door flung open and I threw her up against the wall. Then I licked her face like a giant lollipop, feeling perfectly raunchy all over . . .

"Okay, sweet tits, here I come to save the day."

"Be gentle" she said, her eyes demurring. "It's been a long long time."

I hauled her over to the bed. Then I gave that chick the super-screw of her young, sad life. At some point, I think I sprained my wrist.

Afterwards, I pulled her down from the ceiling fan and we climbed in bed. I tried to sleep but Super Heroes don't sleep too much. I get about two or three hours a night. Insomnia comes with the job.

So I woke her up and crammed another one in. Minutes later we screwed again. And again, until she pleaded for a modicum of mercy—or at least some lubricant.

Eventually I drifted off, feeling much better about myself, about existence, life, and even the world, as well as my place in it.

It went on like that for days. Some mornings, I needed icepacks for my lower back.

Yes, my initial interest in Chai-Lai had been physical, sexual. Animalistic. A convenient means of therapy, maybe even a sick attempt at revenge on Lois. But the problem with people, I've found, is that when you spend enough time with someone, you start to realize that the person you're with is human and has feelings, thoughts, aspirations, dreams. I find it's pretty hard to avoid caring about any decent human being, even when you try like hell to avoid developing feelings, so you wind up with this unintentional and unwanted attachment. I mean, all I wanted was a one-night stand. Maybe a two-night stand, with very little standing. But I guess I'm not cut out for it.

As the weeks slipped away, I came to appreciate Chai-Lai's gentle ways, her kindness and understanding, her intrinsic moral worth and goodness, her gentle joy of life and soft-spoken warmth. Lois had been the love of my life. And I knew she'd always have a place in my heart, so to speak, but our entire relationship had been overwrought with intellectualism, riddled with academic disputes regarding the attainability of a unified system of ethics, of super-ethics, and mired, too, with a competitive spirit that colored our friendship with a constant tension that wasn't always healthy.

Chai-Lai, on the other hand, she didn't lecture me on my responsibilities toward humanity, toward global warming and crime and education and all the rest. Chai-Lai wanted only to be with me, to be near, to share simple pleasures while helping to heal my damaged heart, my broken self-confidence, my lost faith. She didn't bother me about Russian cartels or nag me about disarming this or that nuclear arsenal.

No, she had absolutely zero desire to compete with or confront me, wishing only to make me happy. Chai-Lai, in a word, was good. Good with a lowercase g. No aspirations for the notion of greatness, with all of its tension and moral murkiness. Just goodness. Simple goodness. And her simple goodness helped to palliate my pain, to slowly heal the twin sickness of cynicism and disenchantment. She was building me back up, making me much stronger than before, maybe stronger than I'd ever been.

I am, perhaps, in love.

Yesterday, Chai-Lai took me fishing in the morning and then we rented jet-skis in the afternoon. In the evening we shot pool at an outdoor bar and watched the beery sunset. I could've used some sunscreen, but otherwise, it was a perfect day.

We got back to the Marriott and Chai-Lai lit some scented candles while I called down for room service. Afterwards, we screwed like Macedonian pornstars, then passed out in a puddle of our own glorious filth.

In the middle of the night—or, technically speaking, early in the morning—my Black Berry woke me up. A business call. I never should've picked up, but I did. I stepped out on the balcony to take the call so I wouldn't wake up Chai-Lai.

It was some bureaucrat calling from the Hall of Justice, asking if I was available for a call-out on a routine bank robbery in Oakland, where the cops were on strike—or not on strike, exactly, but many of them were calling in sick at the same time, as a means of renegotiating their contracts with the city. If I refused this call-out, reportedly, I could no longer remain in "paid status." I'd be placed on some unpaid sabbatical, more or less.

Nope, I said. Wrong guy. He pleaded. No thanks, I said curtly, and then I followed that up with a text reply: **Call Captain Marvel or that other no-load, Green Lantern.**

When I returned from the balcony, stepping through the sliding glass door, Chai-Lai was propped up in bed watching a local news channel that I couldn't understand (all these super-powers, and the only language I can speak is English). She looked up from the TV with a tender though suggestive smile . . .

"Put your costume on," she said, stealing one of my smokes from the nightstand.

"The whole thing? I mean, how would that work?"

"No. Not all."

I got the general idea. So I stood there at the foot of the bed, wearing only my red cape and yellow belt. She told me to service myself, right then and there, to demonstrate how quickly Superman could get wood. I thought this rather strange at first, but I obliged. Gave it my best. I nearly had smoke coming off the thing. Sometimes I don't know my own strength—I'm just glad I didn't yank it off. She was impressed. *Amused* is probably the better word choice here.

Then it was my turn to give the orders. I was dying to see it all. Up close and personal, in a way that prudish Lois would never allow.

Chai-Lai's eyes, they watched me watching her as I told her what to do . . .

"Lie on your back," I said. "Now open up those tan, sinewy legs of yours. Wider, *wider*. That's right, girl, show it to me. "

I dove face first into that marshy paradise, my tongue doing ten thousand r.p.m.'s. She went nuts. It was a like a remake of *The Exorcist* dubbed over with a Thai accent. She spoke in tongues. I threw a great big super-load inside, feeling ten pounds lighter and all the happier about existence.

Oh, and it just kept on like that! Until the sun came up!! Until there was nothing left in us to give. I mean granted, there's no such thing as bad sex; but, when you're with someone you really care about, and that person seemingly has boundless reserves of enthusiasm and energy, it's pure fucking magic.

Aquaman was right. Thailand was exactly what I needed.

Earlier this morning, we ordered room service and lay around, snuggling, touching feet to feet, smelling each other's unwashed bodies.

I was starving. As we waited for breakfast, Chai-Lai rubbed some aloe on my sunburn, which basically covered every part of my body except my pupils.

While I was brushing Chai-Lai's hair, the food finally showed up. At least I thought it had. I answered the door, but there was no one in the hallway. I looked left, then right, and then someone clunked me over the head with what felt like a Weber piano.

When I came to, Chai-Lai was gone and I was tied to the bed, Gitmo-style: naked, with a glowing green boulder of kryptonite strapped around my neck. My vision cleared; Batman came into view, standing over me with that sententious air of his.

"Oh," I said. "I should've figured."

"The other Super Heroes, we need you."

"For the last time, Batballs, you are not a Super Hero. Okay? You're just, I don't know, a bored rich white guy with lots of gadgets."

"Great. Here we go again. The Big Blue Boy Scout wants to cut me down by defining away my status, which is obviously heroic, super or otherwise. O-o-o! O-o-o!, I'm so hurt! Boo-fricken-hoo. Look, call me whatever you want. A rose by any other name . . . you know the rest. That's not why I'm here, as you very well know."

"Blah blah blah."

"Will you stop feeling sorry for yourself and grow up?"

"How'd you get here, Delta or United?"

"Fine. I can't fly. Let's not be a prick about it, all right? Just this once?"

"Whatever. Where's Chai-Lai?"

"Paid her off."

"I should've figured. You're such an ass. We were really getting close."

"Don't flatter yourself. She seemed happy enough with the dough."

"So where's your Brokeback buddy, Boy Wonder Nuts?"

"How many times have I . . . we're just very close friends."

"Whatever lets you sleep. Can you at least untie me and remove this glowing brick of death?"

Wonder Woman came swooping into the room through the balcony, looking sexy as hell, nearly twisting her ankle as she landed on the other side of the bed.

"We won't untie you until you promise to come with us," she said, still a bit bitter, I think, because I blew her off during the staff Christmas party, back when I was still engaged to Lois.

"I told you guys when I left," I said, feeling bitter about being kidnapped, and also feeling weaker by the minute, "I'm through fighting crime. No one appreciates us. And as for the really bad guys, we couldn't even find Bin fucking Laden, let alone Lex 'The Pecks' and his merry band of thugs and goons."

"That's sort of why we're here," said Batman, at which point Robin leapt from the closet where he'd been hiding.

"Superman," Boy Brokeback said to me, lisping the first letter of my job title. "Your little Lois? Sorry, handsome, but that wasn't Lois."

"Huh?"

"That ice queen you were living with for the past year," said Wonder Woman, "was actually Lois-zarro."

"The who?"

"Bizarro Lois," said a voice from some unseen corner of the room. "It was a plot hatched by the Legion of Doom. That cunt was just a stooge. They knew how whipped you were, and what a devastating impact it would have on your work, if Lois ever left you in the dust."

"Invisible Man? Is that you?"

"Who else?"

"Jesus, how long have you been here?"

"A week? Maybe longer."

"I thought I heard someone snoring last night when Chai-Lai was on the toilet. I just thought my mind was playing tricks on me but . . . wait. So, all *week*?? You've been watching me all *week*, you voyeuristic pervert?"

"I never would've guessed you'd be so into leather."

"I asked him nicely to keep an eye on you," Wonder Woman chimed in, assuming her typical role of matriarch. "Let's focus on the task at hand here, people. And boys, please, let's watch the language?"

"Right," I said. "So . . . So, if the woman who left me wasn't Lois, then . . . ?"

"The real Lois was kidnapped by Solomon Grundy," said The Flash, just then showing up, still out of breath from running across the ocean after missing his connection in Hong Kong. "She's okay, she's fine. Don't worry, but we do have to—"

"Solomon goddamn Grundy???" I couldn't believe it. "I thought he was dead."

"Apparently not," said The Atom, crawling out of Batman's codpiece, then quickly returning to his normal size.

"Oh, well that's just fucking *perfect*. Will somebody please get me loose already? I'd rather not die here, tied up on a hotel floor in Thailand. I think Carradine already covered that ground."

Aquaman finally showed up, looking under-slept and hungover, completely debauched, and I daresay satisfied . . .

"Dude. Have you seen that Youtube footage of Lois yet? The one titled Lois(dot)Hostage?"

I felt suddenly seized with panic. "Why, did they hurt her??"

"No, no. Nothing like that. It's just, well, The Joker. Man, he's got her all dressed up like Hitler and he's forcing her to sing show tunes from the original production of Cabaret."

Boy Bi-Wonder started prancing around. "Cabaret! That's my fav! You know what? In this one instance, the screenplay is actually better than the original play. Much better story arc. And of course there's Liza—"

"Let's go," said Hawkgirl, removing that fricken kryptonite from my chest, thank Christ, and handing Wonder Woman her lasso, which of course I found strangely arousing.

I got to my feet, still feeling shaky for various reasons. "I'll meet you guys in the lobby. I need to shower up and settle the bill. Plus I feel a super-dump coming on."

"T.M.I.," said Wonder Woman, rolling those big blue eyes.

"Great to have you back," said Batman, playing with something on his tool belt.

"Bro, you mind?" Aquaman grabbed the last can of Singha out of my mini-fridge. "That was one ball-buster of a swim. I'm through with that madness for a while. So um . . . Wonder Hotty, where'd you park that little see-through jet of yours? I need a lift."

"It's over by the naval base. We'll have to take a cab."

Flash quickly did the math. "Will we all fit?"

"In the cab or the jet?" said Bobbin' Robin, seeking clarification.

"The jet," said Plastic Man, whose membership in the Justice League was temporarily suspended for making a trilogy of rather interesting Gonzo porn that was not, in the end, wholly absent of artistic merit.

"Well I know I'll fit," said The Atom, already shrinking down to the size of a gerbil, now standing on Robin's shoulder.

Aquaman called shotgun, adjusting his tight green speedo.

"Not likely," said both Wonder Woman and Hawkgirl, nearly in unison.

"Well, I know Boy Bun-Buster is riding bitch," I said, offering a challenging glare to Batbreath as I searched the sock drawer in vain, looking for my wallet.

"You know that's really not fair," said Robin, launching a typical hissy fit. "Why do I always have to ride the hump?"

"You really have to ask?"

"How come you can't just fly yourself around?"

"Kid, you ever screw all night, smoke a whole carton of Marlboros, and then wake up with a brick of kryptonite strapped to your chest? I didn't think so. Well, you know how you feel after one of your week-long amyl-nitrate binge parties where you wake up missing an eyebrow, a tooth, *and* your underwear? This is ten times worse."

"You're a dick," said Batman, wrapping his arm around my shoulders. "I love you, but you're a dick."

At last, I found my wallet under the bed. All the cash was gone, but there was a pink piece of paper inside. A note from Chai-Lai: "Miss you!" That's all it said. Next to her signature, she had quickly written her number and email address, apparently in haste, before Batbrain had scared her off, or bought her off, or whatever.

S

So far it's been a bumpy flight, with lots of turbulence, in a tiny plane without a single bathroom or so much as a candy bar to eat.

As I write this, during our 10-hour journey from Thailand to The Hall of Doom, all I can think about is Lois. And Chai-Lai. And Lois. And Chai-Lai. I feel so confused, so torn and utterly powerless.

Sure, I've been given many gifts. Who could say I haven't? The ability to fly faster than a speeding bullet, the super-human strength, the X-ray vision. The leaping of tall buildings. This statuesque penis that stays hard for hours on end. Yeah, yeah. I know. All these amazing superpowers and yet . . . I guess what I really want is what most people want: the ability to lead two lives. At least two lives.

As Wonder Woman fiddles with the GPS, I lean forward a bit, and softly I confess to her, "Hurting someone you love is unnatural. But so is monogamy. What're we supposed to do?"

"Your breath stinks like beer, cigarettes, and sex. Go back to sleep."

Warming Up
(Part 2)

Fumiko slams her book shut and stands up with a virulent trill of laughter that seems to say "Well buddy, I hope it was worth it." She seems ready to say or do something venomous. But then she doesn't. She huffs and puffs and leaves the café instead, pushing the stroller furiously.

Fuck, she has the keys! Oh, and our daughter.

—Fumiko, wait, I say through a handmade megaphone—You shouldn't read over people's shoulders in the first place! Hey! Fumi—

Fuck it.

Too late.

Gone.

Flowers and so-sorrys to follow shortly.

When the marital dust has settled, Pam crawls out from under the table with a gooey smile and, much to my chagrin, tries to kiss me.

—What in the hell do you think you're doing? I'm finished, in case you didn't notice.Why are you still here?

Goddamn, that hurt! Bizarro Pam must've been wearing a ring (or brass knuckles). But I'll probably never know; she just stormed out of The Oglethorpe Café and is now crossing the street . . . stark naked and livid, by the way.

She jerks half her face over one shoulder and screams—Asshole!

Nice. Very original, Pam, I think to myself as she bobs down the sidewalk through a steady stream of students and parents, middle-aged tourists and baby-faced marines. Oh look! Our dunderheaded fleshbot forgot her little red bathing suit. We'll be keeping that for old time's sake, thank you very much.

Even though Bizarro Pam—the cultural grandmother to Miley Cyrus—is gone, you can sense her presence out there somewhere, sucking IQ points like a black hole so dense that even light can't escape its insatiable grasp.

So. Who's next?

Ah fuck it, it's just not happening. I've been slapped across the face . . . I've chugged an entire pot of coffee . . . chewed a whole pack of gum for addicts . . . pissed-off my lovable, eavesdropping wife. And you still don't have the first line of a truly workable story. This time, maybe we should cast the male lead first.

—Garcon? Garcon! I say to the sweaty white billboard that is the waiter's back.

—Sir? he bleats, but it sounds like "sure" because of the underbite.

—You sell cigars here?

—No sir, but across the street—

—Am I across the street? No. I'm here. And if I don't get some fucking nicotine fast I'm goin' Columbine on this joint.

—Very well, sir, very well. Although such comments are irreverent and in very poor taste to say the very least, naturally I shall instruct the busboy to retrieve a selection from the tobacconist, he says. Then, with a rather pathetic obeisance, he adds— Immediately.

—Nifty, I reply sardonically,—Bring me back one Bill Clinton along with, all right?

—But sir, Mr. Clinton is *not* an actor. If you're building thematic unity into our story, then I would suggest . . .

—Politicians . . . actors, I say, shrugging my head to one side,— Let's not dive any deeper into semantics here, okay Numbnuts? Tell ya what. I need Slick Willy pronto, and a nicotine I.V., steady drip now, to hell with those cigars.

—Understood. As you wish sir, Numbnuts says, and then scrambles back to his hole.

At this point, I realize that derelict waiter of ours never bothered to bring out the main course.

Next?

A tall, well-fed character with the unguent mien of a successful used-car salesman strolls in, brandishing a perpetual boner and hurling winks as though they were confetti. With one hand, he's pushing the trolley for my nicotine I.V. The other hand's jamming the last of a Big Mac into his face.

I welcome Bill to Savannah and express to him my shocked appreciation for having made it here on such short notice. With his mouth still full of greasy pseudo-food, he tries to say that it's great to be here and offers me his hand. We exchange a few pleasantries, then he sits down with a Cheshire grin.

And now Bill's lolling about, recklessly shifting his weight this way and that on the same chair in which Pamela once sat, with one hand down his pants and the other hand on my shoulder. We make a little small talk, do Bill and I, about certain oaths, you know, and that trail of bodies of course, and about wagging-the-dog, you understand, and oh, just the usual chit-chat while our numbnutted waiter does his best to get the I.V. going.

Bizarro Bill exudes a certain reticence in relation to the topic of Bizarro Bill . . . humble in this regard, I suppose, and so he steers the conversation back to me saying,

—Well, well, well, my devoted supporter, my staff informs me that you're trying to subpoena your inner-dickhead . . . is this correct?

—Th-a-a-at's the ticket, I say. I can feel myself blush as I push through this sort of nervous euphoria. Finally, I get it together—Thanks soooooo much for the support, Bill. I just want you to know what an inspiration you've been to . . . to all of us, you know, who . . . who must embrace the phony within. You taught me; excuse me, I'm a tad overwhelmed. You taught us that there's really only one sin which is—

—The truth.

—Yes! *Exactly* Bill. Now I realize that honesty is a false virtue. We can do whatever we want. As long as we lie or at least deceive. You've proven it, repeatedly. And now I see this in art as well as life. I mean . . . sniff

Bill hands me a white handkerchief. Wiping my tearstained face, I say—Bill, you're the exemplar, the lighthouse, the beacon. And I just want to say thank you. Really. Thank you.

—My pleasure, Bill says with an impastoed grin. Then he puts his arm around my neck, leans forward and whispers—Mr. Loyal Constituent, is little ol' Fumiko all by her lonesome right now?

I decide to lead him on a bit. I explain to Bizarro Bill that Fumiko indeed is home right now, is alone right now, and is angry with me because of a, uh . . . propinquity to certain delicate matters of (shall-we-say-?) a rather lubricious nature. Once Bill has a rough sketch of the situation, I write down an address on one side of a beverage napkin and quickly scrawl a rough map on the other side (for my own amusement, I just gave him directions to the Cathedral of Saint John the Baptist). Bill unwittingly folds the votive, shoves it inside the breast-pocket of his suit-jacket, and, with a crooked, ear-to-eye smile of anguished anticipation, he takes one step toward the street.

I point to the needle in my arm and offer Bill a hit,—You know, a little somethin'-somethin' for the road, I say. He respectfully declines but some vicarious impulse persuades him to squeeze the I.V. bag, throttling the urine-colored liquid into my bloodstream. Now I'm one giant endorphin, one human-sized nerve ending, a giant immortal cock, yearning for the skyward labia of our Creator. (Wait, what the hell was that supposed to even mean?) With a satisfied wink of complicity, Bill takes his leave and disappears, slouching into a cigar shop across the street.

The sun's directly overhead now, feels like a luminous anvil being dropped on my head from the sky. Repeatedly. And yet, the story unfolds . . .

Another Lame Hospital Drama from the 90's

(Only This Time with a Surprising Twist)

FIRST **we need** to finish up the casting. Right. So, the role of Dr. Clooney has been filled by an actor who greatly resembles George Clooney. Officer Pitt, as discussed separately, has already been cast. And his on-screen wife, Britney, has also been taken care of.

We found a Leonardo look-alike to play Nurse DiCaprio. A younger Leo, with a fresh pretty face, still unstained by maturity and professional growth as an actor. This leaves only the role of Nurse Roberts, who—depending on the uneven efforts of our casting agent—might actually get filled by Julia herself. But how do I . . . *wait*.

You know, sometimes it's easier to start at the finish and work backwards, as though cheating a maze. Now then. Let's consider the penultimate scene, located at some extraordinarily ordinary café, something like the café featured in the opening scene of 'Pulp Fiction.' Britney, with a vacant smiled tacked to her face, she'll be wearing cut-off jean shorts, too much make-up, and a Mickey Mouse wristwatch. When the scene opens, Officer Pitt will be sitting across the table from Britney, bulging through his too-tight police uniform. Britney's hands, perfectly manicured, will rest on a big round belly because, by this point in the episode, Britney will be eight-and-a-half months pregnant.

Pitt will make some obvious reference to their marriage having been the product of a shotgun wedding. Then he'll proffer some unoriginal yet sufficiently mollifying comment like:

"But baby, I've never been happier in all my life."

"Oh Brad," she'll moon. "Me too. I've never been happier in all my—Oh,Oh,Oh!" she'll say with a gasp. Her water will break on the vinyl booth; someone at the neighboring table will shriek while a teenager retches and a busboy drops a tub of dishes.

SCENE-2:

Officer Pitt storms through the glass automatic doors of the Townsville Hospital Emergency Room. In the same way he might normally shout, "Police, put your hands in the air," Officer Pitt barks at a pretty male nurse. "Get me a wheelchair, now!"

Insulted but obedient, the frail unfortunate nurse complies.

"What's wrong?" says the male nurse, rolling a wheelchair over to the police officer.

"Wife's gone into labor," says Officer Pitt, then he zips outside to retrieve his wife.

Dr. Clooney leaves a young black half-back with twisted testicles behind a blue curtain in order to attend to the hullabaloo.

"Leonardo, what's going on out here?"

In answer, Pitt wheels Britney to the doctor's feet.

"Ah," Dr. Clooney says. "Who's your doctor?"

"Dr. Aniston," Pitt replies. "But she's in Finland for the weekend. We're early."

"I see. Then I'm her fill-in. Leonardo," he turns to the pretty male nurse, "fetch Julia from the bathroom."

Leonardo zips through the scrub area to the restroom.

Dr. Clooney extends one hand to Brittney.

"Take my hand. Try to stand if you can. Sir, I need your help."

They hoist Brittney onto a bed, caged with metal bars. Dr. Clooney makes three futile attempts to raise the bed.

Leonardo returns. Right behind him is Julia, with a blanched face and no lipstick.

"Julia. Get that boy a bag of ice and some ibuprofen. Leonardo. Can you get this goddamn thing to work?"

Leonardo bites the inside of his cheek to keep from laughing; he wrinkles his nose at Dr. Clooney. Then Leonardo repeatedly taps a button on the floor with his foot. The bed goes up and up.

"Sir," Clooney looks at Pitt. "When's the last time she ate something?"

Pitt thinks.

Leonardo takes Britney's vitals.

"We ate breakfast," Pitt says. "But she skipped lunch because her water broke right there in The Wagon Wheel over on B Street. So, maybe eight o'clock. My name's Brad, Doc, call me Brad."

"Okay, Brad. Is this her first?"

"Baby?"

"*Yes.*"

"Yeah, sure is."

"Anything we need to know about Brad?"

"Nothing special. We did the whole Lamaze thing," Pitt smiles tenderly at his wife, "Breathe baby."

"Doctor," Leonardo says, "BP's one-ten over sixty-eight. Temp's ninety-nine."

"Pulse?"

"Sixty-eight."

"Good. Get me a read on the fetus."

Leonardo manhandles enough gadgetry and wiring for a Kid Rock concert.

Brad and Brittney, they engage in some extreme hand holding.

"Brad," says Clooney, "what week are we in?" *Silence.* "With the pregnancy."

"Oh, uh."

"Thirty-nine!" Brittney belts.

"One-forty," Leonardo chimes. "With variability."

Dr. Clooney explains to Officer Pitt, using an empathetic yet clinical tone, that many visually unpleasant things are about to occur and that, "Just so you know," those fathers who linger in the waiting room will usually choose to leave at this juncture.

"Don't you dare leave me!" Britney says, clawing at her husband's face.

And so our hero, Officer William Bradley Pitt, remains stoically in place. Yes, he stays right where he is and watches this total stranger, the doctor, grope his wife.

Pitt has sworn off swearing, "with the baby coming and all." So every other muttered word is *friggin'* or *effing*.

The pain subsides. Things seem stable for the moment. Britney eats ice chips and walks around a bit. A waiting game ensues.

***

The half-back with the twisted testicles is upstairs now, awaiting surgery, unaware that his uninsured status will financially ruin both his mother and his mother's brother.

Britney is experiencing contractions every five minutes, lasting three minutes. Julia's back in the restroom again, wondering what terrible thing she has eaten to make her feel like this.

Pitt showers his wife with kisses and I-love-yous. Britney sweats a lot. She pants. She looks increasingly worried, sensing, perhaps, that pushing out a life will push her own life through a strange and frightening portal, one leading to a completely unknown existence.

Leonardo shouts across the room to Dr. Clooney, who's stitching two halves of a bottom lip back together for Mister James Carey (an erstwhile barber cum self-employed furniture-mover, also known by meaner folks as 'the town drunk.')

"Doctor," Leo shouts, "BP's one-twenty-four over seventy-eight. Fetal heart rate's still around one-forty. Temp of ninety-nine."

"Pulse!"

"One-ten. I'd say her pain has spiked to a . . . seven, or an eight."

Britney cries out, "Let's call it an even ten!"

"Leonardo. Get her started on Nubain, seven milligrams. Twenty-five milligrams Phenergan, if she gets nauseous"

Britney groans, "Thank God in heaven. Praise Jesus."

"Baby?" Pitt stitches up his eyebrows. "I thought we were gonna go the natural route."

"Are you out of your mind??"

"Um," Pitt looks down at the speckled tile floor, then back to his wife.

"Breathe Baby. *Breathe*."

***

Brittney dilates, then dilates some more. She feels overcome by a bewildering mixture of delight and dread, headed up the first hill of the world's biggest rollercoaster.

Dr. Clooney swabs her cervix and perineum with betadine.

Suddenly, Pitt sees a blob of grey cottage cheese gushing out of his wife. He's between fainting and throwing up when Dr. Clooney holds up a handful of this stuff.

"You see that Brad? There's some green discoloration in here."

"Um," Pitt covers his mouth.

"I'm afraid this means the baby could be under some duress."

Pitt averts his eyes while Leo administers oxygen to Brittney, who now looks like a lab experiment. Meanwhile, Dr. Clooney irrigates her uterus with saline.

***

OKAY folks, we're seeing contractions every two minutes now.

The pain is—well, Britney believes the world might be ending and vaguely recalls an article she recently read in a woman's magazine about near-death experiences. Might she be seeing that big blue tunnel? She can hear herself groaning involuntarily.

"Doc," Pitt tugs at Clooney's sleeve. "Can't you give her something stronger for the pain?"

"Brad, shut it. *Please.* The baby has a decelerating heart rate. Leonardo. Drag Julia's ass of the toilet and have her notify the on-call pediatrician. Tell her to get the surgical team on standby too."

Leo shuffles to the restroom.

Pitt bleats: "What's . . . what's going on here Doc? Come on, what is it?"

"Britney," Dr. Clooney says, "Listen to me. Look at me. Listen, there are some indications that we may have to perform a C-section."

Brittney screams. Her body lurches. "A C-section? But I work at Hooter's, and we need a second income now more than ever. Are you sure? A C-section?"

"Possibly. Just relax. And when you get a contraction, hold your breath. Maintain pressure for as long as the contraction lasts."

Leonardo reappears and checks the patient's vitals while his eyes take surreptitious sips of Dr. Clooney . . . that chin! Those eyebrows, deep enough to grow soybeans in!

Brittney glowers at her husband:

"Brad! A C-section?? That'll make my body totally ugly."

"Baby, they could hack off your nose, and you'd still be beautiful to me."

Leo restrains a sarcastic comment.

Julia finally emerges from the restroom, as white as a bed sheet, and then promptly hops on the phone.

"Leonardo," Dr. Clooney motions. "Let's get her on her L-side."

They roll the patient over.

***

By the time Julia announces that Dr. Jackson, the pediatrician, is on his way, the fetal heart rate has stabilized. A tense calm fills the room.

Leo stands beside a gleaming tray of medical weaponry, gazing hungrily at Dr. Clooney.

Pitt runs his fingers through Britney's damp hair, now the color of wet straw.

Julia self-medicates herself for diarrhea and depression, then loiters uncomfortably behind the doctor.

Push.

Push.

And Britney's perineum bulges with life.

"Julia. See if you can raise Dr. Jackson on his cell. Tell him not to bother coming in. Same goes for the surgical team. Leonardo, scalpel."

Dr. Clooney makes one precise slice, connecting the twin holes between Brittney's sweaty, quivering thighs.

Julia jumps back on the phone, stands-down the surgical team and reaches Dr. Jackson, who's already in the parking lot. Then Julia scampers back to the restroom with both hands pressed against her buttocks as she howls in disbelief at the perfect storm within her bowels, "Ooo-Oo-weee!"

Before Dr. Clooney can issue the order to push harder, a bloody baby is wriggling in his ready hands. Officer Pitt peeks over the doctor's shoulder and weeps, and wails, and blubbers, and he is so beset with joy that his face appears to be in agony.

"I love you baby. Oh, I love you baby. I love you, *I love you*, I love you," he murmurs into his unconscious wife's ear.

Julia returns from the restroom, shaky and reticent. As soon as this is over, she's decided, she *must* go home. It simply can't go on like this. She never should have agreed to that shift-swap; nor to Taco Bell.

Finally, the baby screams and gasps for air.

"Congratulations Brad," Dr. Clooney lifts the bloody lump into the air. "It's a girl."

Dr. Clooney clamps the umbilical cord and hands the bloody infant over to Leo.

"Brittney? Baby?"

"That's all right, Brad," Clooney places a hand on his shoulder. "Let's let her rest a while, she's had a busy day."

***

As Leonardo washes the newborn infant, one thing becomes frightfully clear: this is a beautiful non-white baby. Or rather, this is a beautiful half-white baby.

Naturally, Pitt tries and tries to convince himself that he is seeing something other than what he is seeing. Stunned, Dr. Clooney wonders how he should handle the paperwork, in light of the circumstances. Leonardo begins to chuckle. He does not mean to, but he does. Pitt unholsters his revolver, so shiny and menacing. Shit runs down Julia's leg and into a comfortable white shoe, specifically engineered for long periods of standing. Dr. Clooney raises his palms, as if being placed under arrest:

"Brad, no. No, please. I can see where you'd be upset Brad, but this is not the—"

"Where is he, Doc?"

Silence. A deathly silence, like something from a Bruce Willis movie, in which the only remaining cables on a suspension bridge are about to snap. Julia faints. No one even tries to grab her on the way down. There's this sickening sound of a giant head slap on the tile floor, yet no one moves an inch.

"Well," Pitt says, "Where's Dr. Jackson?" Silence. "You need to get that hearing checked, or what?"

"I don't, I . . . Brad, I," Dr. Clooney stammers hysterically. Leo leaps between the doctor and the gun. Officer Pitt cocks his weapon, a gesture which Leo cannot help but find strangely erotic.

"I know Jackson's the father. *Christ*. And she swore they were just friends. Hm. It doesn't take a top-notch detective to figure out what happened here. Ooo man, that nurse really smells to high heaven. Now you people better talk, or else."

"Oh, you brute!" Leo screeches. Dr. Clooney licks his dry,

tremulous lips and embraces Leo not with lust, but with something much deeper, as he bargains for their lives.

"Brad, he, he . . . he's no longer employed by the hospital. He's been let go. And I can assure you I—"

One

Two

Three

Four

Five shots ring out.

Reload.

And six more shots ring out.

Warming Up
(Part 3)

Um. **So** I uh, really hate to sound like a total softy here but . . . in all honestly, I'm a bit depressed. A bit put off by what I, myself, have written. A shootout scene combined with childbirth doesn't exactly resonate with my sensibilities, such as they are—in fact, this exceeds my own staggering comfort level, which, obviously, says a lot. I guess I need to pull it back a bit or . . .

Well I didn't know where it was all headed beforehand. In general, the mind is a mystery (no honest scientist or philosopher could tell you with a straight face what the mind even is, exactly). And imagination itself remains an enigma within that mystery; I mean, the pen just sort of moved around the page like it was a thin, discount version of some Ouija board. Not that I can be totally blameless here but . . . I'm just saying I would never *consciously* sit down to write something like that. That's all. Granted, I overshot the mark. Let's please leave it at that.

I guess I was just looking for something more . . . unfettered . . . honest . . . raw . . . or pipe-hittin', you know? Yes, that's the word. Or phrase, or whatever.

Pipe-hittin'.

Frantically,

I tug at the waiter's sweat-laden shirt and cordially entreat him—
Garcon!

—Sir!

—Samuel L. Jackson. On the rocks. Fuck it, neat. Oh and my food too, at some point. If it wouldn't be too much of a bother.

(I am, it's true, a product of the 90's.)

Seconds later . . .

Bizarro Sam erupts onto the scene with a tray full of food, looking severely pissed-off, as though roused from a deep deep sleep. S.J. at his peak. Straight from his Pulp Fiction days. He dumps a steaming plate of curry-rice down the front of my shirt and gives Fumiko's club sandwich to a neighboring couple, a tallish redhead with one foot in a cast and her stumpy, cross-eyed boyfriend.

Standing akimbo now, and two inches from my face, Bizarro Sam eyeball-fucks me for a singular stretch of time. I can feel this sort of . . . I don't know, dry tightness in the throat that makes it hard to breathe or swallow. Suddenly, Sam yanks the needle from my arm and throws the entire I.V. rig across the street—narrowly missing Bill, by the way, who just left the cigar shop and is whistling his way through the park now, heading toward a catholic church without knowing it, mistaking my hand-drawn map for something that would lead him to Swingersville.

Tight little balls of panicked sweat pepper my forehead—partly because my "precious" nicotine is no longer drip-drip-dripping into my bloodstream (precious!), and partly because Sam's wearing this facial expression that makes you wonder if he's holding a mouthful of Justin Beiber's shit.

Obviously, I'm frightened. Frightened isn't even the word. But it's more than just fear that's hastening my heart. I really wanna connect with this guy. I want Sam to think I'm hip, that I'm "down" . . . that I know what's up. For once, I want some goddamn validation. I mean, this guy's been a demigod in my mind for so many years that I'm blushing like a school girl on the brink of a filthy confession.

So I try to seem friendly yet reservedly masculine at the same time; I clutch myself and say—What up my brutha?

—Ain'choe brutha muthafucka, says Bizarro Sam with that trademark fury, clearly appalled by my inadequacies, spit flying from his lips.—The fuck *you* want?

Now this is it. This is what we needed. I can feel this sort of, I don't know, hot effervescent surge of testosterone, like a skein of concertina wire being pulled through my veins to the surface of my skin. And I'm ready to stop a speeding bullet, or at least do something rash. I throw my chair backwards onto the deck and lurch to my feet, declaring—That's what I'm talkin' 'bout, muthahfucka.

—Well give me some then bitch, Sam says to me in a way that's cool, calm, but somehow sounds like shouting. We bump chests affably and exchange a few cordial head-butts; I'm thinking, Christ, that fucking hurt, but I know I need to stay in character. We engage in this really intricate handshake that ends abruptly when my thumb gets badly injured. I hope it's just a sprain.

The redhead with the broken foot leans over, offers us some lengthy medical advice regarding the thumb. Samuel drains the last of my coffee, then cuts the tall redhead short. He says a few poignant parting words, slips on some shades, and slides on down the road with these svelte, almost catlike movements. Then he turns around and beckons me with a friendly smile.

—Fuck you waitin' for Scotty? Come on!

As I step off the curb, the street opens up like a giant paved vagina and swallows us whole.

>>>><<<<

Well this is . . . unexpected.

I'm in the Tudor Room, on the third floor of the Indiana Memorial Student Union Building, in Bloomington, in the middle of the limestone campus of Indiana University, where Nostalgia tells me I spent five of the best years of my life, and where I came back to get married nearly three years ago, after Fumiko was pregnant the first time; in fact, this is where our wedding reception had been held after a longwinded ceremony at Beck's Chapel. Wait . . .

The reception's going on right now. I recognize all this stuff. It's a weird scene. Like the second-to-last scene in Our Town, with all the dead people watching the living.

And there's Bizarro Bill and Sammy J., together on the dance floor, with Pam serving as a kind of lunch meat between the two. Everyone else is doing the Electric Slide. The Electric fucking Slide? Did I really let them play that shit at my wedding?

What's this? A new and unexpected guest? Bizarro Dubya, he suddenly materializes wearing a designer cowboy hat made from the ears of baby seals (a fashion that perfectly suits our forty-third president, as anyone will tell you). Dubya tries to cut in on the action, tries to squeeze in on Pam. I snag a beer from the bar and approach them all, the whole writhing mess. Dubya's yelling now, his face the color of Chianti. If he doesn't shut up soon, Sam'll break a foot off. Guaranteed.

Bill takes a step backward, half scared, half smirking—I didn't lay a finger on her Dubya, just try to relax for once. Take it easy.

—Like hell, ya godless pile-a-slime. Lemme tell y'all somethin', says Dubya, fuming.

—Hold up, says Sam, stepping between the two.—Just hold the fuck up. It's Scotty's wedding day, so just be cool. Let's pipe down. Keep this shit on a lower octave and follow me.

Sam bolts toward the restrooms. Bill and Pam, they traipse after. Meanwhile Dubya, arms folded, remains pouting on the dance floor, gawking at the boozers while feeling somewhat disgusted, somewhat sad, and somewhat jealous. Sam returns, urging him along with a few words and a kick in the ass. The foursome disappears through the door to the women's restroom. Naturally, I follow after.

When I come out on the other side, I realize I'm in a big army tent, Korean War era, like the kind you might see in old M*A*S*H reruns. When Pam went through that portal, she must've been cloned. I can see about fifteen or twenty Pams in here. It's crowded.

Bill passes me something to smoke while Sam gets the music going in the corner. This thing I'm smoking, it's like a muffler made from paper mâché; it's bigger than a baby's arm. It burns a hole in my lungs, makes my head tingle. I've never actually done this before and so I cough out a blue cone of smoke.

—So, I say to Bill, —You inhale this time?, then I pass it back to Sam.

—Oh, most certainly, my friend. Though of course I'll deny it faster than a Christmas goose would run for a . . . Lost my train of thought. Anyway, you know what Scotty? I joke, but it's only a coping mechanism. I really did wanna do my best by the American public. The people, I should say. I really fucked things up. I should've chopped off my pecker right after my first inauguration. History'd be calling me one of the greats, if I hadn't gotten bogged down in that whole mess. Or mess*es*. But still . . .

Motown tunes hiss on an old turntable but I can still hear Dubya struggling to read something to four mooning Pams; a short passage from The Gospel According to Exxon:

—Thou shalt only kill evildoers of color who obstruct thine nation from gaining her next petrofix, and if, in the process . . .

Yep, that's House of Saud, Chapter Two, Verse Eleven. Heard it all before . . . global warming is a scam . . . Jesus loves shotguns . . . only the 1% know best . . . blah-blah-blah . . .

Sam approaches me from the side, throws an arm around me. Bill does the same from the other side. We sing together and do a little chorus-line kick to "Tracks of My Tears."

Suddenly there's one Pam on the shaft, another one on the bag, and yet a third Pam behind me, doing something weird, something I refuse to acknowledge let alone discuss. But it's nice, I like it . . .

♪So take a good look at my face . . .

Suddenly, out of goddamned nowhere, Fumiko storms in wearing her white wedding dress. As in real life—as she had been on our actual wedding day—she appears visibly pregnant. She jerks the veil back and shows me two red, puffy eyes. The three Pams who'd been servicing me so sedulously, they suddenly turn their brain-dead attentions to Sam and Bill, thereby leaving me alone with a very pissed off wife.

Fumiko's English is good but not great, considering the fact that she studied the language from the age of six. When she's angry, she still speaks Japanese and I still reply in English. I suppose it's a way of empowering ourselves, a way to shoot from the higher ground.

—Is this what you want, you baka?, she sneers in Japanese.—You want other women? You think I didn't read your old stories??

—What stories?

—Story like this one!, she spits, switching over to English, You still in loving her??

Dinner for Two

(Part 1)

On roads of gray ice packed with new snow, my stepfather's ancient Ford Taurus trundled ahead like a hay wagon behind a jackass. The suspension was shot. The tires weren't far behind.

I thought about Jemma Gerber. Eight years, three months, one week, and five days had passed since I'd seen her last. We exchanged letters twice a year, on our birthdays. Real letters. Made from paper, with texture and smell. Over the years, we've generated thirty-five of these missives in all, seventeen of which were lightly perfumed.

Where Belmont crosses Washington, the traffic light was out of service. Dead or dying cars littered the curb like bugs in a fumigated building—ticking and twitching, futilely starting and finally stopping, as motionless as history.

Funny thing, idle time. As I drove, my mind regurgitated memories, fobbed me with silly happy endings, alternate histories. Rising up through this sea of reveries, both real and imagined, was the trenchant fear that Jemma might not show. I rooted around for my phone. STOP. She's married now. Hearing HIS voice might send you over the edge, if you haven't slipped off unawares already. Then, a new fear. What if, because of the weather, the restaurant has closed down for the evening?

Suddenly, I was enveloped by a rich, melting sense of relaxation, like the kind a heroin addict must feel on his first day out of rehab when, at long last, he can jab himself again. A great big dopamine dump. Nature's **H**. G o o d stuff. It's okay, I realized. She'll wait in the car and smoke cigarettes the shape of pencils . . . if she still smokes.

¿

Enrico's was open. A lonesome yellow flag stood on the table I'd reserved near the fireplace. We certainly didn't need a reservation. As it turned out, the mustachioed waiter and I, we were the only actors on this GarlicMeatballSmelling stage.

A wave of cloying nostalgia stirred me violently, sent me to the toilet vomiting. I had one hand on the cold tile floor. With my free hand, I disconnected ropes of saliva from the corners of my mouth. My nerves were shot.

I cleaned up, then ordered a bottle of red table wine to settle my nerves while camouflaging the stink of vomit in my throat. An hour collapsed. No Jemma. No call. I flagged the waiter.

'Excuse me, what time do you close?'

'Ten-thirty,' the waiter grumbled, without a trace of servility.

'Another bottle of red?'

'Same stuff?'

'Sure. Whatever you gave me last time.'

The wine finally arrived and, with it, my determination to remain until the restaurant closed. I needed something to gobble up the leaden-footed chunks of time. Rummaging through pen caps and crumbs, finally I found a Graham Greene novel at the bottom of my bag. But I couldn't focus long enough to read more than a chapter or two.

Instead I turned my paper placemat over and, pen in hand, began spewing the madness you're reading now. When my placemat was filled with words, I used what should've been Jemma's. When that was filled, I filched placemats from neighboring tables. And then I rummaged through my bag in order to locate and reread all of our old love notes, which were prefaced by a page torn from a journal I gave up on years ago—the failed diary of a failed life.

SWEETEST OF ALL

Back in college I wound up in this art appreciation class. The professor, an Algerian, didn't speak English very well, and she mumbled a lot, and her handwriting was terrible, and I was taking the class on a pass/fail basis anyway, so I really didn't learn too much. Not from the prof, at any rate.

But I did meet someone. Jemma Gerber. She was studying biology. I was studying chemistry, and we certainly had some. Someday, we'd both be hotshot surgeons. Well, that was the plan. We were freshman.

Jemma and I, we joked and teased and laughed until our faces hurt. She was a gold medal smartass but she was also caring, genuine, and fragile at times. And intrinsically lovable. Did I mention beautiful?

Anyway. She gave me a nickname, Frooky. Frooky? The word must've come from somewhere, and when Jemma first uttered this word, it probably made sense somehow. But after a while, neither one of us could remember where it came from, how it had started. Just one of those silly nicknames that can evolve until it only signifies itself, I guess.

Like I was saying, the prof was slightly more animated than the frozen corpse of an ancient stoic. So after a week or so into the semester, we stopped paying any attention to her lectures and started passing notes. I saved a few.

Frooky,
Thanks again (and again and again) for helping me with that quantum stuff. I owe you. Big time. But first,

Will you be my Valentine?
YES NO
Circle one,
Jemma
Ps How old AM I? (snigger)
PPS How DESPERATE am I?

Earthling,
I'm not a mere piece of paper. I'm an alien in the form of a piece of paper. And I'm currently having sex with your fingers. Smile if you enjoy it.
Ah-ha! I knew it!

Much Like,
Zor
PS Only high school football coaches say "big time."

Dear Zor,
I am writing you to tell you that . . . oh wait . . . oh my goodness, hold on (whew). Ok, I'm back now. I had to pause for a second and catch my breath. Wow, I have never had an orgasm in my fingertips before. The feeling just spreads all over.
Tell me, what is an alien like you doing in the form of a piece of paper like this? Do you come to this side of the galaxy often? What's your sign? Do aliens have signs? What are you doing for Valentine's Day? I was hoping you could materialize and take me out. BIG TIME.

More Like,
Jemma

Beautiful,
Sorry I missed class Wednesday. verslept. I was dreaming of you and didn't want to wake up. Now I'm sitting here in class and writing you instead of taking notes. The sacrifices I make for you, I tell ya. I didn't even have a pen: I took one off of Dr. Bennabi's desk. I am such a clepto.

W/B,
Elvis

Dearest Hunk O' Burning Love,
You are forgiven for missing class (but still need a spanking). Now you must forgive me . . . I cannot take my eyes off of you long enough to write. You make me so hot the devil in me is sweating. What is the deal w/ V-Day? Oh yeah, here is something one of your ex-girlfriends would think:
Get it?

NBL,
Pricilla

Scrumptious,
I have to check with my other girlfriend before we make plans for Valentine's Day (joke). How are you by the way? If you're half as good as you look today, you're styling . . .
Roses are red
Violets are gone
What kind of underwear

Do you have on?

W/B,
Richard Millhouse Nixon

Dear Tricky Dick,

You are not a crook . . . at least that's what I keep telling my friends.

Oh sick! The kid sitting in front of me just dropped his retainer on the ground and put it back in his mouth . . . again. That's so . . . high school. Have I told you that you make it easy to get up in the morning? Just thinking about seeing you here in class makes me . . . mooooah! (=loud kiss, get it?)

I don't pray enough but when I do I pray for you. I pray God will give you more of what you want and less of what you don't. I pray he keeps you safe and happy. Oh, and I pray that he (or she!) will make you believe in him or her someday.

Have (you) I ever (want) told you (only) that I (me) love the way you chew your pen? How did you like my little subliminal message, buried in parentheses? Did it work?

I love your notes. The girl with the big hair behind me always tries to read over my shoulder to figure out what I am laughing at. I think Dr. Bennabi is a player. Or a playerette. Whatever. What kind of a teacher wears a skirt **that** tight to class?

Hmm, what color am I wearing? I am not wearing any. Just kidding. In your dreams pervert.

Look, my frooky/yummy/crunchy bacon bit . . . I keep bugging you about V-Day because if we don't have plans, then I need to work because I really, really need the money . . . but I will take the whole day off just for you (if we do have plans). Plus I need to know what to wear, so let me know what's going on. PLEASE.

Hey, can I treat us to some coffee after class? Bookstore?

Tons of Like,
Gypsy Rose

Ms Lee,
Love your work. Now, why do nipples get hard when it's cold? What purpose in evolution could that have ever served? Maybe a better question is this: as a man, why do I even have nipples at all? I'd rather look like a Ken doll. There's just something weird about nipples on dudes.

I keep skirting the whole V-Day issue for a good reason. Please know that, in reality, I'm holding onto your ankles. You didn't notice?

Drum roll.

I procrastinated until every restaurant in Bloomington was already full but: Everything's covered for V-Day. We'll need to skip class. Yes, Jemma Gerber will have to miss class for the first time in her young, suburban life. Monday, the classroom will be darker because of your absence.

By the way, we're going up to Indy. Does a one hour drive count as a road trip? Anyway we're going to the Art Museum, and a play, and a carriage ride, and Enrico's Italian Restauranti, and there you go. So now you know I can't keep a secret. Actually, I'm holding out on one itty-bitty morsel. So don't stand me up.

Hey, get back to me on this nipple thing, it's bothering me.

Your favorite—and only—bacon bit,

Frooky
PS Crunch-crunch :)

Anyway, after countless love notes we graduated to skits and then stories. She would write one paragraph and then I would write one paragraph, and so on. Jemma started with a piece that's now forgotten to time (or at least to me). Then I started up a piece called "Johnny's Ambition" or "Thoughts from a Sperm Cell" or something along those lines . . . I still have several variations of the same story . . . all of them similar . . . but none of them sharing an identical premise . . .

JOHNNY'S BLIND AMBITION

(Part 1)

They share a beer-breathed kiss against the wall while Angel Sanchez roots through his jeans for the dorm room key.

The door flings open, spilling light from the hallway into the room: lacrosse sticks, a pizza box, deadhead candles, beer cans, movie posters, mounds of clothes, two bunk-beds and two desks, sitting opposite one another. Rain pings against the window. The door slams shut.

They kiss and stagger their way to a stereo below the window. The thick end of a middle finger punches PLAY. A very loud Bob Marley fills the room.

Wet clothes eagerly gather into piles. One crisp movement between his finger and thumb sends a pearl-colored bra to the floor with the rest. Now the panties. Slanting through the blinds, moonlight makes her skin appear cadaverous. Impatiently he gropes her young, firm, inexperienced breasts. A mutton-fisted hand drags her first-semester-freshman body over to the bunk beds.

Shit, he says.

What's wrong?

Sheets are in the washer down the hall.

Angel slides her body onto Joe's bottom bunk, his absent roommate's bed. Now Angel lingers above her, committing to memory the moles, the elongated bellybutton, the knobby knees, the protuberant pelvic bone with its modest little tuft—minor but

63

significant differences needed in order to distinguish her from the last, the next, the others.

Each kiss grows more desperate. Knowing hands explore her body. The little dam breaks: diluted honey envelopes his fingers. Her open mouth makes a gasping sound. He takes possession of her hips and then—to the hilt.

No time is wasted. He pummels her body as if with a cudgel. It sounds like a baseball bat being whacked against a side of beef. Repeatedly.

This violence seems so incongruous with the sugary flattery and playfulness of Angel-Five-Minutes-Before that she cannot put a name to what is happening. Her thighs draw together to dampen the slap, the sting, the whack. A knock at the door,

Hey, turn the music down.

♪Old pirates yes the rob I

Angel! Turn it down!

♪Sold I to the merchant ships

Turn the music down, you dick!

♪Minutes after they took I . . .

With her feet flat against the top bunk, her thin legs form a crumpled V, like two anthers of a quickly wilting flower. He grunts; first quietly, then not. Midway through the last stanza of collisions, she cums silently, and seemingly against her will. His hips rummage around in a languid state of de-escalation.

He detaches himself, mechanically, with a satisfied sigh. Squat fingers frenetically search the bed-sheets. He grips her shoulder,

Where's the condom?

The what?, she says, snapping out of it.

Where'd the rubber go?

What do you mean?

I'm speaking Japanese??

Stop . . . being mean. *Please.*

Where'd it go???

I don't know. It's . . . it's dark, Angel.

Well . . . whatever.

Hold on, I'll help you look.

Forget it. I'll worry about it later, in the morning.

But—

It's late, I'm beat, let's crash.

Angel reaches down for a cotton blue blanket, his roommate's blanket. Now the narrow bed forces them onto their sides. She puts a hand on his forearm. He turns away, jamming her back against the wall. Their bodies are moist with sweat and rainwater.

Marley's music finally ends. Only raindrops and breathing fill the silence. There is, in her caress, a plaintive tenderness that makes him ill. So he stumbles from bed. She calls to him,

Where ya goin?

Takin a piss.

***

Midmorning.

Consciousness arrives in layers. Some sadistic force pounds the inside of his skull. He can't swallow. Pinheads of beer-sweat bead up along his naked body. His dry pink eyes fix blankly on the white ceiling.

This room is foreign: a single round table, three chairs, a lamp with its naked bulb, and the gray loveseat on which he is sprawled with a crumpled lampshade behind his head—apparently, a makeshift pillow.

He sifts through the chards of the previous evening: the pre-party in the room, all those glow-in-the-dark stickers, the fight outside Kilroy's, the party at the Beta house. Then his mind reaches the edge of a vortex. His jowls salivate in pre-vomit anticipation. Something has gripped him; a vague sense that his own self-hatred will never wash away what happened in his youth, that's it's all been futile, sad, and all together regrettable.

Vomit rises up, almost to the top of his throat already. Angel shoots up, shuffles to the door, and stops—suddenly aware of his nakedness. He dresses himself with two cushions from the loveseat—one in front, one in back—and waddles to the dorm's communal restroom, which stinks of bleach.

The first wave of vomit, then another. Yet another. More still, until nothing remains but acid. Then, only sound. Finally, not even that. Leaving both cushions by the toilet, he lumbers to the sink and slurps water from a bowl of hands.

Mixed-gender voices in the hall remind him of his nakedness.

He waits. He thinks. Using an industrial ream of brown paper towel, Angel swaddles himself in a disposable toga, then scurries down a vacant hallway toward his room with the single hope that the girl—Jenny—will not be there.

Jenny is not there. Neither is Joe. There is no one whatsoever in this room, including Angel. The door is locked,

Are you shitting me? Are you serious?? Son of a fuckin bitch!

Angel trundles down the hallway, now down a half-flight of stairs, out of the limestone building and into the sun. He walks around the side of the building to see if he can access the second-story window of his room.

A prickly row of bushes stands between Angel and the limestone edifice. This can be gotten around. The window is high but not too high. The windowsill looks large enough to grasp and grapple upward with.

Young men in a jeep drive by, whistling and shouting obscenities. They laugh at Angel, at his paper towel toga. Angel sprints toward the building, leaps, and reaches for the windowsill.

With a reckless jerk, the window screen pops free. Angel falls backward onto the bushes, which devour his paper toga. Smarting from tiny cuts and indignations, he whimpers to himself,

Jesus Christ, can you give me a break!

In a desperate rage, he bounds up the wall to the windowsill. His body flops half-in/half-out of the window. He scrapes himself along the limestone ledge, then tumbles into the room and onto his stereo. The impact of Angel's torso on the stereo compels Bob Marley to resume.

♪Here little darling, don't shed no tear . . .

A sprained ankle, a twisted knee, a chipped tooth, a black eye: these are the injuries for which a young man might prepare himself. But never this. Angel looks down at the fresh and bloody hematoma on his manhood, and he nearly slides into a clinical state of shock.

Aghast at what he sees, he locates a pair of boxer-briefs on the floor and puts them on. The cotton fabric clings to the ooze; it fuses with his wound. Pain. Like a ball of fiberglass shot into your eyeball with a cannon.

So. He removes his underwear and attempts to turn off the stereo. The PLAY button is broken clean off and the POWER button seems hopelessly jammed. He unplugs the stereo. Sweet silence descends upon the dorm room . . . and is shattered by the phone. Might be Keefer with the stuff so,

Yeah?

Angel, she says.

Click.

Ring-ring.

Ring-ring, ring-ring, ring-ring—

What?

Don't hang up. Listen.

All right, I'm listening.

It's about last night.

I know Jenny, I know. I don't know what I was thinking. See I never do stuff like that, and I guess I was just so embarrassed I—

Angel!

Weeping, Jenny mumbles incoherently into the receiver. Something like a fresh polyp of human emotion crowds out what he intends to say. Instead,

I'm . . . sorry Jenny. I'm sorry. Could you please speak up? I'm sorry, I-I can't hear you.

I found the condom.

Found it? Like in your purse or—

No, not like in my purse. Like inside me.

Inside????

Yes. When I . . . went to the bathroom.

How is that possible?

I don't know. It was your—anyway, we were both pretty drunk last night.

A sustained pounding at the door grows insistent.

Go away!

What??

Not you Jenny, sorry. Someone's pounding on the goddamn door.

Well listen, Angel—

GO . . . THE FUCK . . . AWAY!

Police! Open up!

Shit Jenny, let me call you back.

What? Why?? Who's there?

The cops.

Who???

The fucking cheese is here. Can I call you right back?

Police! Open it up before we kick it in!

You're such a liar.

Jenny, I swear to God I—

Click.

Angel opens the door, the same door at which a bowling ball of a man had been charging. The long arm of the law makes a Charlie Chaplin entrance. This short round cop slowly rises from a pizza stain on the floor. Three more cops file in. The last one closes the door. Sgt. Bloom, the nametag says. Icy-blue eyes peer from a don't-waste-my-time face; the sergeant's gaze soon settles on Angel's mangled manhood with more than just a prick of curiosity,

Okay cowboy, you wanna tell us why you didn't answer the door?

Sorry sir. Had an important phone call. Is there something I can help you gentlemen with?

Angel covers the wound with his hands. He tries to smile but his cool is cracked by the day's events as well as the presence of a sizable marijuana plant in the closet, inches from Bloom's flaring nostrils. Bloom appraises the room with disgust,

You live here?

Yes sir.

Got some ID?

Yes sir. If I may get dressed?

Forget it. Had a report of a break-in, but I guess . . .

Perhaps next door, officer. I'm sorry for any confusion.

Bloom nods his head toward the door. His subordinates exit the room. Bloom shuts the door. Bloom opens the door and pokes his face in,

Looks like you need some kinda ointment on that thing.

Bloom slams the door. Chuckles fade down the corridor.

Angel picks up the phone, then realizes that he does not know—and does not even have—Jenny's number. He bangs down the phone. He picks up the phone:

Campus Information, can I help you?

Yeah. I need the number for Jennifer . . . Nevermind. Forget it.

To his injury Angel applies a cold squirt of Joe's lotion. And then he notices something, a few scraps of paper that his roommate had put together. Part of a play, or a screenplay, or what have you, featuring a character by the name of Angel. Though in agonizing pain from his injuries, when he sees his name in print like that, he feels overwhelmed with curiosity . . .

Spring Break

ACT II

Scene Three

Lobo's beach bar: *noon. A wooden outdoor deck with tiki torches. The ocean is ostensibly located where the audience is. ANGEL SANCHEZ is a large, well-built young man around twenty years old; he is wearing shorts but no shirt and is in possession of a large can of beer. BILLY BRAUN is also around twenty years old but notably smaller than his friend. He wears sunglasses, shorts, a baseball cap, and a plain white t-shirt. He is chain-smoking off-brand cigarettes. The two young men are seated at small plastic deck table.*

ANGEL [*rapid-fire speech with rapid-fire gesticulations*]: Yea bro, so I'm gorilla-fuckin this chick over some, some random piece of motel furniture, and like all of a sudden, I hear Dré's bitch losing her shit [*in a diminuitive falsetto voice*] Darius! O Darius! [*laughing*] and I'm thinking, bitch—his name is André. Should've thought of that, switching my name like that. Funny shit. So Dré wraps things up, you know, chucks one in there; whole fucking room's caving in like a bad bomb shelter. Off the top rope. Yeah and Blazo got a whore last night, the sleazy fucker. But wait. So anyway, these bitches had like, a tackle-box full of goods. Meth? Fuck meth man; these chicks had shit you've never heard of. Shit they haven't invented yet. These ho-bags bust out their kit and start popping off names like it was some kind of a, some kind of a, chemistry class for

70

cutting-edge lab drugs; one-three-dimetho-fry-your-fucking-brains-two-three-nitro-blah-blah-blah. Whatever. I was like god*damn* people, you got the shit that killed Elvis; let's ease into this thing, I tell 'em, tryin real hard to hide my Vag-o-sillness. Course, there is no easing; ease, fuck. Shit gets weird. Outta hand. Whole fucking room starts to melt like a box of crayons but it's all good, bro, cause I've got this raging stoiker . . . the size of your fucking thigh, man. My cock was fucking throbbing, dude. Throbbing. So much blood down in that thing I should've passed out. Blazo man, what the fuck? Getting laid here's like trying to throw a rock in the ocean, I mean it's not exactly. Whatever. Can you believe . . . ? [*Leaning in.*] That desperate no-load fucker drove out and bought himself a whore. Two whores, but still man, you believe that shit? Paying for pussy on Spring Break. Course I told him, whores mean dick as far as the contest goes. Zero points. Against the rules. Not stated maybe, but kind of, implied, right? I mean it's like paying for air, or, [ANGEL *takes a drink from his can of beer while he tries to envision something more freely available than air.*] Or—

BILLY [*removing his sunglasses*]: Angel—

ANGEL: Oh and you won't believe this shit. Yeah, and so I'm railin' this chick from behind and Dré steps outta the bathroom. He walks up, totally straight-faced, man. Looks my bitch in the eye and says, who's pussy is this? [*Slaps* Billy *on the shoulder*] Who's pussy is this. Holy fuckin' shit bro, without missing a beat she says [*falsetto*] It's *his* pussy. Goddamn right, I tell her. So then I'm working up the world's biggest nut and you'll—

BILLY [*turning his cap backwards*]: Angel, look—

ANGEL: Hold up. Listen. Listen, you're gonna shit and fall back in it. Guaranteed. So afterwards, we all smoke out together. Still under the spell, you know, and gettin stoned on top of that. Fucked me in the goat-ass. Some weird voodoo shit from Haiti. These buds look kind of like hairy red testicles. Smelled like, I don't know, vanilla. Well I'm kinda . . . kinda balled up with this Emma chick on the bed. Then Dré just wedges in between us. I'm like, what the? Dré, he . . .

you know our boy. Totally straight-faced, Dré says, mind if I cut in? So then we're—

BILLY [*pounding the meaty underside of a clenched fist on the table*]: Angel!

Beat

ANGEL [*concerned*]: What's up?

[BILLY *looks down,* ANGEL *puts one hand on* BILLY's *forearm.*]

Pause.

ANGEL: Talk to me. [*Pause.*] Bill. Billy? What's up bro?

BILLY: There's . . . there's something on my cock, man.

ANGEL [*Let's go of his forearm*]: Something on your . . . you sure? I mean, you sure it's not like, some fucked-up thing with your shampoo or maybe just—

BILLY: No. No, something's seriously wrong with me.

ANGEL: You think, I mean, it's uh . . . it's—

BILLY: Angel, it's the herp.

ANGEL: The fucking herp?? *Jesus.* You sure?

BILLY: No. I—I don't know. No. It's not certain. It's what the doctor thinks, though. Who knows. His English wasn't great. I go back this afternoon for the blood results. What am I, who am I kidding man. I got it. I fucking got it. [*Increasingly upset and incoherent*] How the, what the, son of a fucking; what am I gonna do?

ANGEL: Least it's not—I mean. You know what I mean. The alphabet or . . . [*Beat.*] I'm going with you bro. What time's the appointment? I'm real sorry you, that this . . .

72

BILLY: Me? It's not me. Me's not the issue. Me? Personally? Don't worry about me. Don't worry about that. I don't care about that. Little sore once or twice a year; who really gives a frog's fat ass? No, it's not good. I can't say that. Not good but. It's not like I'm losing an arm. Paralyzed. Brain cancer. AIDS. It's not; it's—what am I going to *do* about Elley?

[*Beat*]

ANGEL: Billy I'm . . . so sorry . . .

BILLY: Either I tell her when we get back to school or; either I tell her or else I have to break up with her; I mean Jesus *Christ*. Two years, I've been a good little boy. Two. *Years*. I never so much as kissed another girl. One sloppy hump on the beach and. Christ, what are my options here?

[*Beat*]

ANGEL: You gotta dump her. I'm sorry. I'm sorry, my man, but that's the way. You tell her the truth and A.) she's gonna dump your ass anyway. And B.) she's gonna run her mouth. That's the way. You don't need some broad bumpin her gums about your business all over campus. I don't need to tell you but, this shit's between you and me. Blazo, Scotty, André; they stay in the dark unless you shine the light. But trust me. You gotta dump your girl. Otherwise? Fess up and get dumped, which doesn't make any kinda sense.

BILLY: But Angel I [*beginning to weep and covering his face with his hands*], I love her. I really love her and . . . [*surrenders to a weeping fit.*]

ANGEL [*standing*]: Come on. Come on Billy, let's get outta here. The boys'll be down any second. Come on [urging him by the tricep]. Come on, let's go. Let's go for a walk.

BILLY: [*rises and allows himself to be guided down the beach . . .*]

JOHNNY'S BLIND AMBITION

(Part 2)

The doorknob rattles. A kid with a concave chest and a carroty goatee canters in,

Oh. My. Fucking God. What'd you do to your pecker? Looks like you smashed it in a car door.

Thanks. Door's open. You mind . . . ?

My bad. What happened last night? I came home, totally maggoted, and there was some chick in my bed. So, like . . . ?

Later Joe. Seriously. Not now. And the next time you decide to use me when you write some lame-ass screenplay? Change my name at least.

My bad. Of course I was gonna revise the whole thing, just so you kno—

You have a light bro? I'm dying for a smoke . . .

On the dresser. I thought you quit?

Thanks. Look, I'm jumpin in the shower. Do not lock the door.

***

The showerhead draws a watery curtain between Angel's day-time-self and his inner Mr. Hyde. But no amount of scrubbing can wash away that rat-bitten feeling in his guts. He turns the water on full blast.

Now Angel flicks a cigarette butt into the shower drain. The holes are too small, it won't go down. He sits down on the new tile floor with his back against the wall, his muscular ass muscles blocking the drain.

Water gathers around him, slaps his neck and shoulders. The

cigarette butt floats up, then down to his toes. He huddles his arms around his drawn-up knees. Thoughts of last night, of Jenny, of the prodigal condom; they all conspire to stage a mordant tableau in his head . . .

Daddy, how'd I get here?

Well Johnny . . . half of you waited in Mommy, until one day the other half went shooting out of Daddy at a million-miles-per-hour. Then half of you—Daddy's half—it slept in a rubber halfway house with billions of your half-sisters and half-brothers. That halfway house was supposed to be a tomb but somehow you must've checked out early. Chalk it up to operator error, my boy.

Wow. And what happened to all my zillions of brothers and sisters?

Let's see. Some died in the halfway house of course, or in the toilet I guess, and the rest died on The Trail of Seamen.

Daddy, what's the Trail of Cement?

Well, Johnny, semen is a kind of . . . organic drink. Your naughty Grandpa used to squirt it down Daddy's throat when he was about your age, which is partly why Daddy is so fucked up today. But anyway son, The Trail of Semen was the march to Mommy's egg, which is your other half.

But the rest all died? That's so sad.

No kiddo, not really. That's the fate of most half-people. They die on beach towels, in gym socks, on tampons, up against ceiling fans, and just about any-god-damn-where you can imagine. Billions of these little half-kamikazes—so eager to join this world—they splatter themselves on some strange new surface every day.

But I didn't die, Daddy, so I guess I'm special. Right? What'd I do on the Trail of Cement to make me be so special?

You see Johnny, you were competing with a whole gang of other greedy little monsters. But you beat your tail the fastest, never thinking even once about the consequences, the downside of life. No kiddo, it's not the brightest or the kindest who make it to the egg. It's the one with the most blind ambition. That's you Johnny. You're the unlucky one—you made it to the egg.

Daddy?

Yes son?

You're a real asshole.

Yes son, I've been told that a time or two.

***
**
*

At this point Angel looks up at the showerhead, for the first time realizing that he is evil. Not flawed, wayward, naughty, or simply misguided. *Evil.* Prior to this moment he had considered evil to be something "out there," in the world, or else a small but minority component of everyone, including himself. He now realizes that thoughts and intentions are essentially meaningless alongside human choices and actions, that the choices made in his young adulthood could only lead him to conclude that he was evil, a force that makes life for others worse, not better. Yet realizing this he also realizes that only a person with some degree of remaining goodness could see the evil within and feel revulsion, feel horrid, hollow, less than empty. He hates himself. He hates himself more than he hates any other person or thing on Earth.

As one thought gives birth to the next and the next, Angel grows conscious of the fact that being evil does not guarantee that he should remain so. Perhaps he could change. The realization that he *could* change, and *wants* to change, this marshals in an overwhelming sense of obligation, a sense that it's now or never, that he's reached a fork in the road and that the ramifications of failing to change now, in his youth, will doom him to a life unworthy of being lived. Suddenly Angel Sanchez becomes aware that, for many minutes already, he's been murmuring the same simple sentence repeatedly, with the force and tone of an inward prayer . . .

I can be good
    I can be good
        I can be good
            I can be good
               I can be good . . .

Trick or Treat

NOW the story I'd like to tell involves costumes. Actually, it requires costumes. Okay, that's simple enough. We'll make it Halloween.

Halloween where, exactly? Not really sure. It's gotta be someplace, I guess . . . hmmm . . .

Location.

Location. Midwest? Not too cold, not too hot. Perfect costume weather. But *where* in the Midwest? I keep putting everything back in Indiana. Get away from the hometown lure, the trap, the vortex. I don't know . . .

The story might start in front of a simple row house, maybe along the Ohio River in Cincinnati or . . . or maybe outside a ritzy brownstone, up in Chicago.

Yeah, what the hell, that'll work. Chicago. More specifically, we'll set this thing in Old Town.

Okay. So the POV starts off across the street from this brownstone walk-up apartment in Chicago. Specifically in Old Town, as I've noted. And there's the address: 303 Willow Place.

Yes, and the sallow streetlight mingles with the hazy dusk along porch steps. It's chilly.

ENTER: the trick-or-treaters. A few kids . . . a pack of four or five should do . . . they amble up the porch steps of 303 Willow Place. Make it six. Six trick-or-treaters. Four boys and two girls. We have one angel, one clown, one ghost . . . and I guess the rest are super-heroes. Good enough.

The angel knocks on the door. The boys tell her to use the doorbell. She does. Now a short stocky ninja comes traipsing along, tries to the join the group. Apparently a loner. Apparently not associated with the others. He/she gets in line behind the others.

The chunky red door swings inward. A tallish brunette with an attractive face and big round eyes opens the door. The children clamor. The angel, the clown, the ghost . . . they all get their candy and make to leave. Then the ninja speaks up. He has a queer little voice, like it's almost falsetto or something:

"Ma'am? Can I please use the bafroom?"

"Oh . . . uh . . . goodness, I, uh . . . we . . . "

"Please. It's a 'mergency."

"Where's your mother?"

"She's at work. At the hospital."

"All right. I suppose there's no harm in . . . come in, please. Right this way."

The brunette, Loraine, she escorts the tiny ninja through the family room and, in so doing, comes between the television and her husband, Shawn, who's buried in a somewhat expensive couch with his tie undone. Shawn's face, though otherwise stunning with its fierce angularity, defies conventional beauty because of a large, kidney-shaped birthmark along the left cheek. He angrily musses the bangs of his spiky blond hair:

"Loraine! The game! What are you doing? You promised if I let you do that Halloween horseshit, then there wouldn't be interruptions."

"Sorryyyyy."

"What's that kid doing?"

"He needs to use the restroom."

"Well hurry up then. You're killing me here. You have any idea how much money I'll lose if the Bears don't wake up in the second half?"

Loraine, muttering under her breath, leads the ninja down a corridor toward a clean half-bath with a white marble sink top. The ninja shuts and locks the door.

Meanwhile, the doorbell rings. More kids. Loraine, noticing that her punchbowl of goodies is nearly empty, sprints to a cupboard in the kitchen to get more candy. The doorbell rings again. Nearly knocking over a costly lamp, Loraine sprints back to the door where she is greeted by five trick-or-treaters and two adolescent boys who didn't even bother with costumes. She doles out the candy to everyone except the two older boys, the ones without costumes.

"Hey lady," one says. "Where's our candy?"

"Sorry. No costumes, no candy. It sort of defeats the purpose, don't you think?"

"Come on, Mrs. Roland. I used to deliver your paper. I'm Jason Thompson. Don't you remember?"

When Loraine returns to the living room, she screams and drops her punchbowl, which shatters, spitting candy and glass all over the parquet hardwood floor.

The ninja, who's no longer wearing his hood, and who for some reason is choking her husband with a piano wire from behind, looks up at Loraine but makes no effort to loosen his grip on Shawn, whose purpling tongue wags to one side as his eyes roll back with moribund resignation.

>>>><<<<

At this point, the narrative needs some sort of a flashback in order to bring this why-done-it full circle. So here we insert a somewhat unusual back-story (as told from the perspective of the little ninja's wife, Dana).

>>>><<<<

People never seem surprised when I tell them that me and my husband met in the circus. A couple months before they hired Winthrop, my husband, they hired me to be the 'Strong Lady,' which stands to reason when you figure on my size and all.

Winthrop says I pulled him out of the gutter. That's what he says. When we met, I was taken by the man right away. He had a way about him. Our dressing rooms were always right next to each other. But at the time he was going with some perfumed trollop, this acrobat by the name of Nadine. Nadine fell through a rip in the net once and busted her noggin. Her nose was flat against her face and her laugh was as nasal as can be. I can't see what the man saw in her, except they drank all the time together.

Then one night, a foggy night outside Tuskegee, we was putting on a show. It come my turn. I was to juggle three midgets, like always. There was Winthrop and two others. They don't matter. Far as I know, they're still in the gutter. Not that we don't pray for them.

I was juggling the midgets like usual, the crowd was going wild, when all of a sudden, I heard this loud popping noise, then a quiet, puppy-like yelp. It was Winthrop. Come to find out, I had yanked his little shoulder plum out of its socket. He was laying on the ground. Mr. Utterback, the circus director, he come over and told me to get Winthrop's arm back in place. He said the show must go on. My little man looked up at Mr. Utterback and he said LIKE HECK IT DOES, only he didn't say heck. With his good hand, Winthrop grabbed hold of my hand and begged me not to fool with his arm and plus he begged me not to leave him alone. I said I never ever would. I knew we was in love. I knew he knew it too.

The circus was no kind of life. We quit and moved to just outside Chicago, where his uncle was building subdivisions by the truckload. This was back before the bust.

Anyhow, we planned on getting married a year out, except I got pregnant so we got married quick and had a quick honeymoon in Zephyrhills where I could see all my sisters and brothers.

With the baby coming and all, Winthrop quit drinking and gave his life to Jesus. I still wasn't ready. My own father had been a pastor and he was not a very good man. That's how come I wasn't ready.

Winthrop got tired of working for his uncle so he got himself a plumbing certificate. Two more daughters later, I got one too. Now we own a little plumbing company by the name of Big & Little, which maybe you heard tell about. At first it made me sad to see how a lot of folks would call us out to work on their homes just to see what we looked like in person, I mean, after they seen our advertisements on the TV and all. Anyhow, we work real good as a team, what with me being a retired strong woman, plus and Winthrop can fit inside all them tiny spaces.

The lord had blessed us many many times but, just like in the book of Job, I got tested something fierce by the lord our savior. Something terrible started to happen. I started having terrible dreams.

I will never forget the first real scary dream I had. Truth be told, I can never remember the dream, just what happens when I wake up. Anyhow, I woke up in the middle of the night one time and I was choking poor Winthrop almost to death. What with me being big and Winthrop being little, it was a very very dangerous thing to do. The psychologist we went to, she said probably it has something to do with my father. I'm acting out, is what Dr. Lunt said.

By then, I mean by the first time I tried to choke my beloved husband, we had three daughters. There was January, February, and April. But anyways. After that first dream, there came others. I was so scared I would hurt my dear little Winthrop, what with my doing bad things in my sleep; after a while, I moved into the spare room down the hall. Winthrop didn't like that. Not one darn bit, but he understood.

Then, when I come to think about it, I was scared I would harm my babies too. I just could not be sure what I might do in my sleep. So I moved all the way out to the garage. My heart and soul ached something fierce for my husband's touch, to lay beside him each night and listen to him snore like a buzz saw. I was a prisoner to my dreams. Heck, the whole darn family was.

All I really mean to say is, Winthrop's fortieth birthday was a very big deal. Only I wanted you to know why. Winthrop had put Jesus first in his life, but once each year, only on his birthday, he was allowed to drink. So that's what he did. He drank and drank. Beer, mostly.

We was in the downstairs part of a fancy bar called the Road Tap when Winthrop handed me a box. It was gift-wrapped. It looked real pretty. I shook it to no avail. I could not guess what was in that box. He said I'd have to think real hard on what the present really meant. When finally I did open up the box, I was overcome with big fat tears of joy. That's when I told my beloved husband that I was all the way ready to put Jesus first in my life. Things was looking up, so far up that, when I think on how the evening ended, it rips my heart clean in two.

>>><<<

THE ROAD TAP PUB, Winthrop's fortieth birthday.

Winthrop eased a present across the table toward Dana, who looked askance at the gift.

"Winthrop," she said, "It's your birthday, not mine. I'm not supposed to get no gifts."

"Honey, you are the gift, the best gift I've ever had, praise Jesus."

"What is it?"

"Take a guess. When you see what it is, you'll need to think about it for a minute. It's very important to me, to both of us."

Dana shook the gift. She shook it right next to her ear. Finally, unable to keep herself in suspense any longer, she opened it.

"Handcuffs?" She looked puzzled.

"Think," he said.

For months, Dana had been sleeping in the garage because, on more than one occasion, she had attempted to choke her diminutive husband in her sleep. Suddenly, she understood.

"Oh, Winthrop," she cooed, and cried, and hid her face.

"It came to me in a dream," he said. "The Lord told me to get you some handcuffs so we could finally be a family again. I'll fasten you to the bed each night. Don't worry, we'll get used to it."

"Praise God, Winthrop. Praise God."

"Baby, you really mean that?"

"I do."

"You mean—"

"Yes, Winthrop. On Mamma's grave, I am ready to put Jesus first in my life."

"Sweetie, you don't know how happy you've made me."

Just then, a pack of bellicose corporate types herded past the bouncer. They glared at the big woman and the tiny man, and they could barely contain their laughter.

"Come on," Winthrop said. "Let's go in the back and shoot some pool."

Winthrop was drunk by then. Dana won the first two games. Three suits walked in, part of the same pack that had been staring at them earlier. One of them, a tall black man, approached Winthrop.

"You mind if we squeeze in a game?"

"Sure, but we just broke. It'll be a minute."

Then one of the suits said something. He was a tall, good-looking man with spiky blond hair and a prominent birthmark on his face.

"Follow the yellow brick road," he said, using an over-the-top Munchkin voice. The other two suits laughed and laughed.

Winthrop ignored them. He tried to take a shot on the seven-ball but scratched. He was too distracted by their taunts. The blond businessman started singing and doing a dance:

"We represent the lollipop guild, the lollipop guild . . . "

Winthrop looked at Dana, then at the suits, and then back at Dana. Dana's eyes pleaded with him to remain silent. But he simply couldn't.

"Look," Winthrop glared up at the blond. "You got something you want to get off your chest? Huh? You got something to say?"

"What??? You must be kidding me."

"I assure your dumb ass that I am not."

"I'm trembling here, Tom Thumb. I didn't know the circus was in town."

"We're not with the circus no more," said Dana, rather missing the point.

"It's funny," Winthrop said, growing cruel in reaction to such cruelty, "being taunted by a guy with bird crap permanently affixed to his face. I guess they call it a birthmark, though I don't see the connection. Are you even old enough to appreciate your resemblance to Gorbachev, dookie-face?"

"You any relation to Tom Thumb?"

"You already used that one, you repetitious nitwit."

"Whatever. So tell me. How is it you can screw that chick without her giant cunt swallowing you whole?"

The black guy in the background, now visibly embarrassed, left the room and went to the bar. The other two suits, they laughed histrionically. Winthrop yanked a pool cue from the wall.

The blond suit snickered. "And what do you think you're gonna to do with that?"

In answer, Winthrop charged him. The blond guy took one long step forward and punted Winthrop into a vintage jukebox in the corner. Winthrop tried to launch another offensive. Dana held him by the shoulders.

"Darlin', calm down. Calm down. This here ain't the way of the book."

"Hell, even Jesus flipped over some tables. Baby, let me go."

"Please honey, let's just go home. Please."

The blond guy egged him on. "You're lucky that big bitch is holding you back, ass-nuts. You scuffed my shoe."

The bouncer, responding to the noise and the gathering crowd, ambled over and asked what was going on.

"Nothing," Dana said, still holding her husband. "We're leaving. I don't think we like your bar."

Outside, along the curb, Winthrop started weeping. The humiliation had been too much. Dana tried to hold his tiny hands. He wouldn't let her touch him.

"Go home," he told her. "Here's some money for a cab."

"I got money but . . . but why ain't you coming home with me? We're a team, you and me. Don't get all bent outta shape over nothing."

"I'm going to the nearest police station. I'm sure somebody in there saw what happened."

It took some prompting, but eventually Winthrop convinced his wife to go home without him.

Then he sat there for a good long while, in a cab with the meter running. When the blond man finally left the bar, Winthrop leaned forward in his seat and stage-whispered to the cabby:

"See that guy? The guy with the birthmark? Follow him to his car. Or whichever way he goes."

The cabby, having been overpaid, gladly followed the pretty blond man to his new black Audi. Then he followed the Audi to a brownstone apartment in Old Town.

"Three-Oh-Three Willow Place," Winthrop said aloud, committing the address to memory.

The cabby turned half of his unshaven face toward the back seat. "You gettin' out?"

"Nah. Not here. Take off. Just go straight . . . okay, turn left here and follow it up to Lincoln Park."

ACT I

Scene Four

3 **03 WILLOW PLACE**. *As the scene opens, six trick-or-treaters approach the door. WINTHROP, disguised as a ninja, follows up closely behind the others. Inside, SHAWN, a young professional, sits on the couch watching a televised sporting match, which can be heard when his wife, LORAINE, opens the door to the trick-or-treaters.*

LORAINE: [*handing out candy*] Here you are . . . here you are . . . and here you are. Happy Halloween, everyone be safe out there.

ALL: [*Departing*] We will . . . Thank you . . . Bye, Mrs. Roland . . . Hurry up, Tommy!

LORAINE: [*sees that* WINTHROP *still remains*] Are you okay? What's the matter?

WINTHROP: [*in a childlike voice*] I need to use the bafroom.

LORAIN: Oh . . . uh . . . goodness, I, uh . . . we . . .

WINTHROP: Please. It's a 'mergency.

LORAINE: Where's your mother?

WINTHROP: She's at work. At the hospital.

LORAINE: All right. I suppose there's no harm in . . . come in, please. Right this way.

[*They cross through the foyer, then into the living room where they block* SHAWN's *view of the television.*]

SHAWN: Loraine! The game! What are you doing? You promised if I let you do that Halloween horse shit, then there wouldn't *be* interruptions.

LORAINE: Sorryyyyy.

SHAWN: What's the kid doing?

LORAINE: He needs to use the restroom.

SHAWN: Well hurry up then. You're killing me here.

[LORAINE, *muttering under her breath, leads* WINTHROP *to the bathroom.* WINTHROP *shuts the door.*]

[*The doorbell rings.* LORAINE *sprints to a cupboard in the kitchen to get more candy. The doorbell rings again. Nearly knocking over a lamp,* LORAINE *sprints back to the door where she is greeted by five trick-or-treaters and two adolescent boys,* JASON *and* JEFF, *who didn't bother with costumes.* LORAINE *doles out the candy to everyone except* JASON *and* JEFF.]

JEFF: Hey lady. Where's our candy?

LORAINE: Sorry. No costumes, no candy. It sort of defeats the purpose, don't you think?

JASON: Come on, Mrs. Roland. I used to deliver your paper. I'm Jason Thompson. Don't you remember?

[WINTHROP, *seeing that the coast is clear, exits the bathroom, then tiptoes behind the couch and begins choking* SHAWN *with a piano wire.* LORAINE *enters the room, screams, and drops a punchbowl filled with candy.*]

LORAINE: Oh my god, oh my god, oh my . . .

WINTHROP: Hold on a second. Before you say anything, listen. Listen, this bastard, a few months ago, this bastard insulted my wife and . . .

LORAINE: You're not a child!

WINTHROP: Yes, I realize that. This bastard insulted my wife and kicked me right where it counts.

LORAINE: Let him go! Get your hands of my husband!

WINTHROP: He would've done the same thing to me if . . . if . . . He didn't know me from Adam. I never did anything to make him . . .

[LORAINE *picks up a lamp and clunks* WINTHROP *over the head.* WINTHROP *falls to the floor.* SHAWN *gasps for breath.* LORAINE *rushes to embrace him.* SHAWN *pushes her away, stands, and picks up* WINTHROP *by the back of his ninja costume. The hood of the costume falls off.*]

SHAWN: All right, you little shithead . . .

LORAINE: Should we call the police?

SHAWN: [*Throwing* WINTHROP *across the floor.*] I remember you, Tom Thumb. So you wanted your revenge, eh?

LORAINE: What are you going to do?

SHAWN: Lorraine, honey, sweetums. Lock the door. I'll be downstairs in the basement until Monday.

ACT I

Scene Five

SHAWN'S WOOD SHOP IN THE BASEMENT . . .

Winthrop's eyes travel from the bloody tips of his fingers, which are now missing their fingernails, to the pliers that did the work, and now to the blowtorch that's ever so slowly approaching his face, realizing for the first time that he'd been drunk on his own self-righteous sense of injustice, that simply being right can never compete with strength, that goodness will never compensate for being small and weak, that in this world of ours, power—raw power—trumps everything — power alone is what determines the outcome of national and personal histories — yes he realizes this but, as the blowtorch inches toward his left eye, he also understands that this realization has come too late to be of any use. As he mentally prepares himself to be blinded and then slowly killed—murdered on the installment plan, if you will—suddenly from the top of the stairs comes the sweet rumbling sound of salvation:

It's Dana, that sweet beautiful giant, wielding a Craftsman 18-inch chainsaw . . .

(to be continued . . .)

Dinner for Two

(Part 2)

Another hour collapsed. Hope was a brown leaf, tumbling toward the turbid steam below. But before this leaf could kiss the water's skin, there came the creak of a door and a cool echo in the form of a draft. Jemma.

Yes, Jemma Gerber . . . inching toward me with the demure deportment of a diffident angel. Never had she grasped her brilliance. Never. Not a day had touched her face. She was A Picture of Jemma Gray, with satin tendrils of pale yellow hair toppling over shoulders too narrow for her overcoat, which years ago had been a Christmas gift from me. One size too large.

Her shiny blue eyes, overwhelmed by the prominence of her pupils, they seized me as those gluey lips framed her piquant teeth in such a way as to form something that was both a smile and a wince.

Noticing her diamond earrings, I wondered if her husband knew that her first-and-only-love had purchased those very earrings ten years before. It's amazing, the mysteries and broken gear we hand off to the next guy.

Jemma edged toward the table. I stood, barely, on two sticks of margarine. Awkward hug? Handshake? God no. Warm embrace? Too bad we're not Japanese, we could simply bow.

Our faces hit like two hot liquids. I can't remember who dove at whom. Nor can I recall the interlude following our kiss. Suddenly, it seemed, we were seated across from one another with a fresh bottle of red between us. Jemma, her coat mysteriously absent, wore the same champagne summer dress I had, on many occasions, indicated to be my favorite. And leaping from my favorite dress: meeting breasts, large enough to resemble a small ass.

'Jesus, Jem. You uh . . . you look great.'

'Thanks. You too,' she said perfunctorily.

I knew she was lying. While the years had ravaged my face, my scalp, my body, and my spirit, somehow Jemma had escaped the great and violent vandalism perpetuated by time. Her eyes plumbed the depths of my decrepitude; they judged how deeply life had cut me in order to count the richness of her victory.

Not a minute later, I was standing over Jemma, clutching a salad fork. I paused. She froze. Without another word, I jammed the fork quite deeply into her neck, narrowly missing her jugular. She didn't seem particularly taken aback, so I repeated the gesture several times.

'Sweetie,' she said, with the fork still protruding from her neck, 'will you please sit down so we can talk about it?'

WHATHUMP. Icepick to the temple. A rivulet of blood trickled down the side of Jemma's head like a bottle of nail polish turned on its side. I brought my face down close to hers and spat:

'You cheated on me, you dirty bitch. Where'd the icepick come from? Some movie. Basic Instinct? Some Like it Hot? Thinking out loud. STOP IT.' Task at hand, keep it together. 'You cheated on me. And that really fucked me up.'

'I know, I know. Now take this thing out of my head so I can think. Please. Come on, let's talk. It doesn't have to be like this.'

'Fine,' I huffed. Her temple made a strange though exquisite sucking sound as I drew the icepick from her head, still fuming at her: 'Angel Sanchez? Angel Fucking Sanchez?? You just had to fuck my best friend, huh?'

'He was so persistent.'

'Yeah, that makes it okay.'

After returning to our opposing seats, we resumed our salutary tête-à-tête. Nail polish gone. Wounds no longer gaping. She took my hands with motherly confidence.

'Baby,' she said to me softly, 'I'm sorry. I am sorry. But you cheated too, ya know. And I know it doesn't make things any less ugly, but I think it's important for us to—'

I reached across the table and did something that, normally, I would never dream of doing. I slapped her face. A 'bitch-slap,' if you like. Then I barked:

'You cheated first.'

'Okay, so um ... What meaning does that carry now? I'm sorry honey, but you make it sound like we're in a sandbox here.'

'What are you saying ... it's all semen under the bridge?'

She released my hands.

'Don't be crude, please.'

'Crude things, Jem. They were terrible, crude things.'

'Yes. They were. So?'

'So you did it *first*.'

'Scotty, not again. For the love of God.'

'Chronology isn't some trivial detail. Not in this case. It's called a chain of causation, in case you're forgotten how to think empirically.'

She looked away—dismissively, I thought—sipped her wine and lit a cigarette, looking all suave and aloof, like some 21st century Ava Gardner. She really had it coming so ...

THWACK. I buried a hatchet along the narrow white part of her flaxen hair. She sighed and, while trying to free the hatchet from her head, took a long drag from her mentholated cigarette.

'Okay,' she said. 'I give up. My sin is worse than your sin. Is that what you want to hear? Happy now??'

'Hey, don't be so glib there sister. You just don't get it, do you? It was the original sin.'

'Oh. I see. So your argument is ... You never would've cheated if I hadn't done it first?'

'Precisely.'

'You're certain?'

Jemma's perfidious eyes pressed against mine. Hers were stronger. They made me question a conviction I'd held for eight years, three months, one week, and five days.

'No. I'm not "certain." I think so though. Give me a break, Jem. You can never be sure about these alternate histories. Certainty? ... What a bunch of sophist dribble. Still, I mean, when you think of it as a probability statement ... When you consider Occam's Razor. You know what I mean, you studied all that stuff. Well honestly, do you think I would've cheated?'

'I don't know. I don't think so.'

Triumphant, I banged my hand on the table.

'There you have it. So you confess?

'You poor simple bore, confess to what?'

'Your dumb ass threw us out of the forest, banished us forever from the Garden.'

'The garden?'

'Eden, if you prefer.'

'Ahhhh,' she tittered. '*THE* Garden.'

'Don't laugh at me. For Christ's sake, don't laugh at me. Have you ever loved anyone as much as you loved me?'

'No. Of course not.'

'Do you still love me?'

'Of course.'

'And we had the closest thing to perfection a human being can ever ask for. Do you understand? Do you really understand?'

She wept into a maroon cloth napkin.

'I do . . . I . . . I know I . . . '

'Then why'd you do it? WHY?'

'Because I was drunk?'

Her narrow shoulders made a flippant little upward gesture that was not at all to my liking. So I leapt on the table and quickly introduced her teeth to the toe of an exquisitely polished shoe. She cried out, then spat a bright dollop of blood onto the placemat. I smiled. She gasped through broken teeth.

'What next?'

I unbuckled my belt with a kind of swanky, hillbilly, Dueling Banjos ascendancy.

'No,' she whispered. 'No, don't. Don't! . . . please. Never stoop so low as to weaponize your sex!' She clasped her hands together as though in prayer. She's right . . . no. I shouldn't, I couldn't, still—

Buckling my belt, I stepped down from the table and sat beside my little buttercup with a soda bottle in my hand. Where'd the bottle come from? Hmmm. "Outsiders" maybe? So now I'm Pony Boy?

I caressed Jemma's back and, with my right hand, smashed the soda bottle on the mantle, then handed it to Jemma. It had a perfect jagged edge. Her big blue eyes grew glassy with dread.

'What am I supposed to do with this?'

'Cut your face off.'

'Cut my—'

'Face.'

'Off?'

'Yes. At this point, it's vivisection or goodbye for you. I've been really pissed about this for a really long time, if you haven't noticed.'

Laughing, I placed a loose tress of silky hair behind her ear, then patted her cajolingly—old-buddy/old-pal—about the back and shoulders.

Jemma hesitated, perhaps going over the options. A moment later, she made her choice.

I rubbed her neck while she methodically carved a chunk from her face, then placed the bloody chunk on a white appetizer plate. Another chunk, then another, as I soared above the very treetops of ecstasy, briefly yet intensely appreciating the joys of cruelty . . . 'the dark side,' if you prefer.

I fed these juicy womanchunks to a pride of kittens, whose paws made figure-eights about my feet. Of course, I tantalized them first. Ah, chunks of my love, dangling above meows. The beauty! The horror!! I rolled Jemma over, face-first, into the clapping jaws of this sandpaper-tongued hydra (NiNe KiTtEnS iN aLL).

O t'was quite a soirée
As cute as two mittens
Nine calico kittens
Nibbling on Jemma Pâté!

Luckily for Jemma, I hate cats. I couldn't stand to see them feasting and purring, purring and feasting on my little buttercup in such unremitting bliss. So I doused her hair with lighter fluid and touched her off with a vintage Montecristo. Woe, fire's spreading pretty fast, I better—Put her out with vomit. Some viscous, opaque stuff. Burned coming up, very acidic that. Remake of *The Fly* I think or—

What had been human was reduced to a mound of bubbling goop, smelling of burnt hair and looking like poop. From the poopgoop stared two big black eyes . . . Beseeching me, they were.

I looked up at the ceiling for a moment and, when I looked back, Jemma was hunkered down on the floor, without so much as a blotch or a Band-Aid, though she was weeping inconsolably. Still, she looked good, all things considered.

On the way to Enrico's, I'd been chewing the question: Can I ever forgive her? But watching her shake and weep like that, I knew the tables had turned. I'd gone too far. She continued to weep. I crouched down beside her.

'Can you ever forgive me?'

'No,' she said with a sob. 'Never. But you can make me forget.'

'Make you forget?'

'You're the writer, sillyhead, you can make it happen.'

That's right. I'm the driver, I can—WAIT.

'You're right, Jem. Actually, I can make you do both. Do you forgive me?'

'Yes,' she said robotically.

'Good. Thank you, Ms. Jemma Whatever-Your-New-Name-Is. I forgive you too, or at least I'm well on my way. What can you remember?'

'About what, silly?' Jemma rolled her eyes, laughed coquettishly, and wiggled her toes on mine. Yes, Mr. Cohen, it's a cold and very, very broken hallelujah.

'Here, follow me,' I said.

I took her hand. We stood, knees first then feet. She studied my face:

'Where're we going?'

'Over here,' I replied, as we skated along the floor of the restaurant, which had turned into a sheet of blue ice. 'In there.'

She giggled.

'Into the fireplace?'

'Yep. Hold on one sec. Just need to jot down a few more lines before we go.'

I plunked a moist sugar cube beneath her tongue. Popped one myself, it tasted like absinthe. While I scribbled the dénouement, we shrank and shrank. Soon we were Lilliputian and could easily squeeze into that fireplace.

'Alrighty Jem, it's time now.' We laced fingers and followed an inverted waterfall of light up the chimney, toward a new land.

ACT IV

Scene One: NEW LAND

Late afternoon. SCOTTY and JEMMA, *festooned with commercialized hippie garb, appear quietly contented, though not exuberant. SCOTTY is perched atop the aft portion of a yellow rowboat. JEMMA is reclined, using SCOTTY's chest as a pillow. SCOTTY appears almost ten years JEMMA's senior. The oars form an X, protruding from the prow of the boat, not utilized. The boat, of its own accord, creeps ever so slowly down river. The upstage bank of the river is lined with tangerine trees. Neither the trees nor anything else on the set looks real (there is a decidedly 'Gilligan's Island' feel to the entire set). In the wake of the rowboat's progress, pools of mercury flotsam periodically give rise to large garish timepieces whose hands turn counter clockwise at a moderate pace. A white scrim, situated behind (upstage of) the tangerine trees, has, via backlighting, achieved a marmalade color by the time JEMMA utters her first line.*

Jemma: How you feelin'?

Scotty: Good, you?

Jemma: Groovy. I really dig this place. Nice breeze. Hey, remember when you wore an afro wig all week to finals?

Scotty: Mmm-hmm. Still have the wig . . . somewhere, I think. Was that actually racist or simply crude and infantile?

Jemma: And what about the time we were headed to a movie down on Kirkwood and you drove us all the way to Graceland instead?

Scotty: Oh, yeah. Yeah, [*chuckling*] that was fun. There's something to be said for flights of fancy.

Jemma: Art class? Passing notes, cracking up all the time. You were always such fun. You really were. You haven't lost your sense of humor have you?

Scotty: No, haven't lost it. I just wonder sometimes if it's gotten a little . . . I don't know, warped? [SCOTTY *cracks a small sad smile. JEMMA yawns and grows visibly drowsy. The prow of the rowboat rises out of the water, followed by the fantail. The boat slowly ascends into the sky. The marmalade scrim behind the trees grows lighter and lighter and should be bright white by the close of the scene.*]

Jemma: Where're we headed?

Scotty: The past.

Jemma: Wow, curiouser and curiouser, my little bacon bit. It sure seems bright. [*From the bottom of the boat,* JEMMA *recovers a pair of kaleidoscope/retro sunglasses and draws them to her face.*]

Jemma: Wait, why the past? So we can meet again and do it right this time?

Scotty: No. So I can unmeet you.

Jemma: That's crazy. Why would you want to unmeet me? [*Yawning, turning on one side, facing downstage, ready for sleep*].

Scotty: So I can love my wife.

Jemma: Oh, that's so sweet. [*This last line is mumbled almost incoherently.* JEMMA *falls asleep on* SCOTTY's *chest while* SCOTTY *plays with* JEMMA's *hair. Exit: Stage Left. What is now a white scrim fades back to marmalade, then to black. During this slow fade, an excerpt of Terry Jacks' version of "Seasons in the Sun" should increase in volume at the same rate that the light fades, beginning with the song in progress "But the wine and the song . . . "]*

CURTAIN

Warming Up
(Part 4 aka "All Warmed Up")

Fumiko . . . **Fumi?** That's a really old story you were reading there. Really old. Like, written years ago, before we even got hitched. Come on, you've got it all wrong. Take a seat.

I sit down on one of the green canvas cots, up against the dank fabric of the army tent, with the muffled sounds of our wedding reception barely audible in the background. Reluctantly, she joins me. Sammy J. corrals everyone out of the army tent. We're alone.

It's quiet.

In the army tent, one of the overhead light fixtures must've been bumped . . . it's still swinging, as if we're riding on a ship at sea. It's at this moment that something takes over, some unseen hand; we're not speaking English anymore . . . we're not speaking Japanese, either . . . We're speaking perfectly fluent Swahili and, for the first time ever, we understand each other perfectly. I think I can rapidly translate our Swahili exchange into English, without losing too terribly much of the original subtext . . .

—Scotty, open up. Talk to me. How can I learn if you never talk? And I mean without using sarcasm as a defensive wall, for once. You want other women?

—Oh, yes and no. Not like how you think, baby. I just want them in my head, that's all. It'd make me sick to ever go through with it. Go back over these pages Fumi; it's just a story about a guy and his fantasies. Plus a little extra. That's all. I guess, well, that's what morality is really all about. It's *not* about what you do in your skull, it's about what you do with your body. Physical, tangible morality . . . it's the best anyone can hope for, I think. I'm totally onboard with Aristotle in that character, true character, is the sum of our choices . . . nothing more, nothing less. The rest is white noise. Who cares what I think about in the shower, or driving down the road between sales pitches? I mean, come on. At the end of the day, you know I've never cheated on you, right?

She nods and sobs and averts her eyes.

—And you know I never would, don't you?

She begins to sway and yank at her hair like a mourning wife at a funeral in classical Athens. A sick, low groan grows louder and higher.

—Fumi, baby, what is it? What's wrong?

I massage the back of her slender neck. Rising to her feet, she rivets me with a fiery, incisive gaze.

—Do you still love her??

—Who?, I say, as my shoulders pretend a shrug of innocence.

—Scotty, I read a whole stack of your old stories. There's certainly—how should I phrase this?—a recurring theme. Not just that one story, either. So . . . ?

—Look, the key word there is old. Sit down. Please, sit down . . . Okay, you want the whole truth and nothing but it? Is that why you climbed inside my skull?

—Yes. Give it to me. Only this once. A hundred percent truth, undiluted by your usual diversions. After this, we can go back to our routine, our quasi-honest arrangement, just like most married folks.

And so I give it to her. What the hell, none of this is really happening anyway, so I lay it on her. I talk very calmly with meaningless hand gestures that seem to amplify my thesis but in fact these gestures are made only because I'm inwardly wrecked and nervous and using these gestures to buy time and gloss over a manifest lack of coherence with regard to meaningful self-expression. I stop for one moment to clarify what seems to be an important point.

— . . . and by relying on the term 'soulmate,' I don't mean to imply any belief in a soul, as such. It's just a familiar term that everyone recognizes. Anyway baby, I just think the 'soul' is like an egg. Usually, it can only be fertilized once. This one fertilization disallows all later attempts to reach the egg. You follow? I don't buy into that romantic crap about 'the one,' I'm just saying: once you've had the soulmate experience, even if it's flawed, subsequent fertilizations might be impossible. Because of biological programing. Or something. Fumi, is this getting through to you?

—Yes. You are saying I am not your soulmate. But . . . I love you so much Scotty.

She starts to weep again. I take her in my arms, squeeze her gently, and inject her with a few more ampoules of truth.

—Baby, I love you too. And you have my respect, which is a lot more than I could ever give a soulmate.

—I am confused. You never respected your soulmate?

—Never. I don't respect myself very much, so how could I ever respect my soulmate? We were just two clumps of shit that got stuck together for a while. Two vultures have a lot in common. It doesn't make them pleasant. She and I, we were shit. Complete shit. And you're the diamond baby, embedded in a hot pile of shit—me. But you'll always be my diamond.

—Truly?

—Truly. Granted, your English is pretty sucky and my Japanese is ten times worse, so there's a sense of loneliness sometimes, isolation. Pent up expression. A sense that we'll never know one another completely, that so much must go forever unsaid. But emotionally? I was an emotional quadriplegic before I knocked you up; now I'm learning to walk. And every day I'm a better person because you're in my life. And I'm happy, sort of. Probably as happy as a guy like me can be. Real love is wanting to fuck other people and never doing it. Real love is the way you lost your inheritance to marry a white guy. And it's the way I sell copy machines, even though every day I wake up, I tell myself I'm going to run away and finish my novel. And sometimes, in the middle of a sales pitch, I really do feel like killing myself.

—Yes, Scotty, real love is sacrifice. And you are. You do. But you do it as a martyr, like a charity, an act of pity, which is sad sometimes and insulting at other times.

—Fumi, I . . .

—Listen, Scotty. I'm not your charity case. Look, moving into a new phase of life like this, it resembles a rebirth. And each rebirth springs from the death of a previous life. Your problem is an insistence on living both as a human and as a ghost.

—Come again, love?

—It would be a lot easier for you to embrace this life if you could let go of the previous one. It's unbecoming. It's immature. It's hurtful to us and to yourself. We enter this world shackled to the demands of our parents and society. As parents, we are shackled to the demands of our children. For a brief period called Young Adulthood, which is mislabeled if you ask me, incidentally, there is a brief illusion of nearly absolute freedom. But it's not real and, historically speaking, it's a complete anomaly. People are *supposed* to be shackled to other people. It's time to face your responsibilities, not like a martyr, but like a man. I love you. I love you so much. But for the sake of everyone in your life, including yourself, it's time for you to grow up. Do you want to do this together, to raise these children together? Are you truly ready for this, or would you rather see me on the first plane to Osaka?

—Oh my God. The fact that you would even ask me that . . .

—Let me ask you this in a different way. If you could do a magic trick and start all over again would you . . . would you be with me, with us?

Rising, I take both her hands and kiss them. We amble toward the opposite end of the army tent. I unzip the two green flaps, then unzip the mesh scrim. We step into a brightly lit waiting room with new blue office carpet. Sitting on sterile grey chairs are several Mes, several Scottys. About ten or twelve in all. One Me is listlessly flipping through an old Time Magazine, another Me is staring blankly at a sports page, another Me is yawning, several Mes are nodding off, one Me is consulting his watch, and so on. I peck Fumiko on the cheek.

—Look around, Fumi. This is how I feel about family life, about my life with you, the life we've chosen, the life to which we have sentenced ourselves.

As you'd expect, she gives me an earnest but poorly aimed left hook, then begins to wail and weep uncontrollably. Now I bend down and fold back a black throw-rug. Under the rug is a nautical steel hatch, which some young sailor must've dogged down very tightly. Finally, it budges. This hatch turns out to be an oubliette that leads to a highly fucked up place. After a while, I persuade Fumiko to lie on her stomach next to me and look down through the little trap door.

Below us we see a medieval dungeon, one where hundreds of Mes are being tortured and eaten alive by various wild animals and so-called forces of darkness. My skin is being peeled from my body; I'm being eviscerated, and vivisected, and made to swallow hot oil, and I'm pushing a boulder up a hill . . . I'm being whipped, and burned, and quartered, and I am made to wear short dresses, and I am forced to read Mrs. Dalloway whilst an emu pecks at my feet. I point to one Me, screaming on a bed of nails that were dipped in "Extra Strength" Ben Gay sports cream.

—But you see Fumi, this would be my life without you. Relativity matters, it always does, and I could find no clearer expression of my love than showing you my waiting room alongside my personalized dungeon. The shit going on down there makes that waiting room muzak sound pretty sweet, right?

Her face softens, just a tad. I shut the trap door and we make very boring but happy love on the new blue office carpet in the waiting room, while all of those apathetic Mes look on with bored but somewhat happy faces. When I finish—which takes a while, because of my earlier sessions with Pam—we hold hands and walk through the tent, through the women's restroom and out to the dance floor in the Tudor Room.

All of my drunken friends, they wave and make lewd gestures; they knew what I was up to in the tent. Sort of.

Now we slow dance to an old mawkish love song called "Woman in Red," even though Fumi's wearing a bright white wedding dress. Why? Well it was sort of our song, because of the way we met. Because when I first saw Fumiko in Kyoto, on the Kintetsu line, sitting in a crowded train next to a middle-aged "salary-man"— which I myself have become—(it was during the *Obone* holiday), she was wearing the most gorgeous red kimono; that's when I approached her and asked if she'd be interested in a free English lesson. Smiling she closed her book, the last finished novel by Osumu Dazai, and the rest, I suppose, is history.

And so I guess no matter how black the past might be, and no matter how grey the present seems, she needs to know that she'll always be my woman in red.

Now, as we dance cheek to cheek, a profound sense of gratitude and appreciation melts over me.

—Fumi, I whisper in her ear—I love you, baby.

—I know. I *know it.*

I consider the possibilities associated with cloning her . . . but then she kisses me softly, and I decide against it. Instead, above her head, I conjure up a glowing halo and then kiss her once again.

Acknowledgements

I would like to thank my wife, for enduring the process, as well as the gang from my Edinburgh days, who helped me hone that process.

About the Author

Andrew Armacost studied literature and writing in Scotland at the University of Edinburgh after serving in the U.S. Navy, during which time he worked at sea and overseas, with long-term assignments to both Afghanistan and Singapore. Mr. Armacost, whose writing teeters between literary and bizarro fiction, has also resided in Illinois, Ohio, Georgia, Florida, Japan, and California. His most recent publication prior to this was *The Poor Man's Guide To Suicide* (Moonshine Cove Press, 2014), a literary novel about the travails of a non-custodial father fighting for his children—and his will to live. Presently he lives in Virginia with his wife and family.

Boiled Americans by Matthew Allen Rose

Boiled Americans is a puzzle box in book form, inspired by the violence of living in urban America and exploding the tendency to forget or ignore.

Great American Slasher by David C. Hayes

Baseball, apple pie . . . and murder.

The Bohemian Guide to Monogamy
by Andrew Armacost

Here, a strange labyrinth of interlinked short fiction assembles itself into a darkly moving novella that deftly explores the bottomless pain and pleasure of love and commitment, the hinterland between youth and adulthood.

Surreal Worlds edited by Sean Leonard

An anthology of surrealistic compositions created by some of the finest names in genre fiction. A showcase of international talent undaunted by the conventions of language and common narrative structures. Here is timelessness. Here is Surreal Worlds

How to Succesfully Kidnap Strangers by Max Booth III

Do not respond to bad reviews. If you must respond to bad reviews, please do not kidnap the reviewer.

ADHD Vampire by Matthew Vaughn

He came, he conquered, he was distracted a lot

Notes from the Guts of a Hippo
by Grant Wamack

A rugged journalist travels to Brazil in search of a missing hippo researcher and the notes left behind lead to something earth shatteringly revelatory.

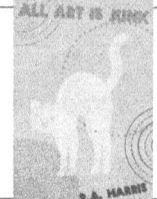

All Art is Junk by R. A. Harris

Lana Rivers, a girl with paintbrush hair, is missing and it's up to Lancelot, her cyborg knight, and his bionic conjoined twin, Cilia, to find her before her evil father, a disrespected artist turned mad-scientist, performs a terrible experiment on her.

Cherub by David C. Hayes

Cherub wasn't like the other boys—too slow, too rough—but he didn't deserve what that hospital did to him, and now he will make them pay.

Skinners by Adam Millard

Los Angeles, the City of Angels. At least, that's what the brochure says. What it fails to mention is the earthquakes. Oh, and the flesh-eating creatures lying dormant beneath the concrete, waiting for the chance to surface once again. Their wait is over . . .

The After-Life Story of Pork Knuckles Malone by MP Johnson

What's a farm boy to do when his pet pig becomes an evil, decaying hunk of ham with slime-spewing psychic powers?

A Lightbulb's Lament by Grant Wamack

A gentleman with a lightbulb for head wakes up in a world full of darkness, hooks up with a beautiful ex-prostitute, and an old man who can heal people; he travels down south to find the mysterious Creator.

The Horror Show by Vincenzo Bilof

A poetry novel—a narcoleptic, amnesiac Nobel Prize-winning poet becomes the subject of an experiment to cure madness.

Beyond by Jordan Krall

From Jerusalem to Mars, psychiatry and the unraveling of the universe

Gravity Comics Massacre
by Vincenzo Bilof

An absolutely shitty novella involving comic books, aliens, a serial killer, teenagers in an abandoned town, horror-trope dream sequences, and an ending you're going to hate.

Glue by Scott Lange

Sticky bowels and sticky situations.

Ascent by Matthew Bialer

Is the 8 foot tall creature haunting a small town in Iowa in the fall of the year 1903 the product of a hoax and collective imagination or was it one of the first documented paranormal event in America? This epic poem grapples with these questions.

Fecal Terror by David Bernstein

A killer turd is on the loose!

The Fairy Princess of Trains
by Christopher Boyle

Danny's mediocre life turns upside-down when his couch starts whispering to him. Then he's charged with a supernatural mission: Rescue the Fairy Princess of Trains.

Terence, Mephisto & Viscera Eyes
by Chris Kelso

9 new science fiction stories from Chris Kelso

Industrial Carpet Drag by Bruce Taylor

Chemicals make you do great things!

Bizarro Bizarro: An Anthology

The finest bizarro short stories from 2013.

Necrosaurus Rex by Nicolas Day

Necrosaurus Rex tells the tale of Martin, a simple janitor, who takes an unfortunate trip through time, becomes a violent mutant, and the father of us all. There's 14 billion years crushed inside these pages, and most of them are pretty nasty.

Day of the Milkman by S. T. Cartledge

In a world dominated by the milk industry, only one milkman survives after a terrible storm sinks all the ships and throws the Great White Sea out of balance.

Moosejaw Frontier by Chris Kelso

An unapologetic disaster of metafiction

The Boy Who Loved Death by Hal Duncan

From blackest humour to bleakest horror, with twisted relish, Hal Duncan's eighteen tales dig into death—and the life that goes with it.

www.ingramcontent.com/pod-product-compliance
Lightning Source LLC
Chambersburg PA
CBHW072033170626
46811CB00008B/3066